DEG

BY
PATRICK GARRATT

URBANE
Publications

urbanepublications.com

First published in Great Britain in 2016
by Urbane Publications Ltd
Suite 3, Brown Europe House, 33/34 Gleaming Wood Drive,
Chatham, Kent ME5 8RZ
Copyright ©Patrick Garratt, 2017

A CIP catalogue record for this book is available
from the British Library.

ISBN 978-1-911129-48-6
EPUB 978-1-911129-49-3
MOBI 978-1-911129-50-9

Design and Typeset by Michelle Morgan

Cover by Julie Martin

Printed and bound by CPI Group (UK) Ltd, Croydon, CR0 4YY

urbanepublications.com

For Fiona

The wonderfully original illustrations in **Deg** were created by *Ste Pickford*. Ste is a full time video game designer, part time comic artist and occasional illustrator from the north of England.

ONE ⸺

Ira Jones born red brick Wrexham building trade. He left school early. A six-month recovery from the effects of general anaesthetic proved challenging, but his back zip fierce magnet to the ghosts and Ouija. Plastic streamers laced bells at the top of wooden stairs with honey tea sweet spread through the mushroom dark like a pack of cards. Rosso weighed the deg on copper scales, his fanning face spider teeth clack.

We took the nipples from the field up Ruabon, said Ira. The wall gave some ponytail opposite.

There's my web, said Rosso, licking up his hairy black legs and balancing the deg against a two pence piece quarter ounce bad deg but better than nothing mixed up. The block left brown stains on Ira's fingers. Grit and perfume web air with pollen and yellow gas ran straight to his teenage balls. Rosso chewed them up. Dew soaked the web. Wooden stairs plastic black Ira lost the garden portal.

Rosso would manage Wrexham's biggest deg house down the funnel, but Ira had yet to learn the aura lessons web-boy. Heavy on the deg and the mushrooms was Ira, a knife-carrier in the woods.

He liked the locking kind with the saw-back in the deer neck and ate badgers in the night showed lights on the grass with the dogs off a-killing. Down by the church through the black on mushrooms. Cockroaches floor bed and the cross of Bersham in the clotted night, dead men and glow down by Delamere lake, dead trees, dead water silver on the face and step-in-step with mushroom Ira.

Someone's with us, he said on the other side of the bush, eyes teary heart bleeding. Jacob gasped ran with him little squeaks, unbecoming for such a large one. Couldn't wank in a room without curtains. Burgundy spliffs as mushrooms wound down on ridiculous Giles.

He blamed the trip, but Ira checked with the spirits and Suzanne touched his hand as she passed the deg. They knew better. Foot slipped from the clutch in Maroon's white van couldn't without a spanner while they smoked deg in the back and the bounce drew Ira up to the top. Jacob shat his pants but Ira and Seamus puffed chests and rode the scares. Seamus black in the corner power melted cream walls and air solid square checkers around his skillet face black corner shifted his black eyes met in the gallery's centre aloft embraced before Seamus glanced down covered cheek glow and went trotting back to Jacob put his arm around Seamus and reached for his little floury prick with the other hand, smiling all nasty at Ira black corner eye. Ira used the pain to talk to the thin walkers.

They couldn't cut the black malevolence from his ribs in Liverpool a piece of bone as thick as a miner's fist and just as cancerous. Cantona kicked a fan in the chest the nurses played it out on the ward wireless. A vultured pensioner bedding next to Ira complained at the noise when the news finished and the music resumed no surprise fucker had a triple bypass looked like death, his chest carved yellow staples crawling with cock-sized maggots. He's our prisoner. Marble guardians allowed family visits but only screeched in ear blue uniforms truncheons. Golf magazine. Stop breathing like that. Boy George fell over the decks. The nurse thought Ira grassed his pill habit to the doctors, his furry speed teeth threatening to up the morphine dose if he cost him his job, but he had Ira wrong. Food wars in his smack dreams. Apache gunships raked the base of the desert cavern ripe cacti all Gulliver. Translucent women sucked miner spunk. Black with Welsh coal better than starving drank the spunk from the miner cock. Scalped crown lionesses and their organs sparkled green and fuchsia, ribbons of electricity yellow on their sea faces and war effort rocks and tanks beamed through their cheeks pushed the button for another hit. Ira wanted more but woke wanted to sleep, said the nurses. Sweeping drillings from the wings semen in the bottle air in the wing factory. Ira hardcore siren on the wing jigs. Doctor Loon prowled the floor below. Acid for blood they showered metal from the drills onto the uprights, seventy-foot monsters fierce on the wings and deg in the Triumph after.

You won't be here tomorrow, said Maroon.

Doctor Loon pulled up in his silver Mercedes and Ira's mother shrank to the kitchen.

Take your shirt off, boy, he said. Ira chewed his lip as Loon sucked his cock, nibbling its tip with filed teeth while he laid maggot eggs in the corner of the living room. Real tasty, said Loon. Time for egg-fucking then back to the wing.

Ira didn't see the point in complaining so took the remainder of his dick and smeared it over the jelly surface of one of the eggs, pumping blood through the flexing membranes. The maggots flashed pink and began to eat each other, becoming larger until a single huge maggot eventually occupied each egg.

Bend over, said Loon. Loon's cock resembled a Buddha with ॐ tattooed in red ink on the head. Finger-thick teal veins circled the shaft. A layer of cottage cheese packed the bell.

Fucky now, he said. Give me the ghosts. Ira opened his ass up like a watermelon revealed glowing insides.

Fuck shit, said Ira as Loon pushed in, moaning as if drowning. Buddha head bigger than a deer skull stretched Ira's colon. Loon fucked him with his grey egg legs. That's it, said Ira. Come on, Loon. Right up to your fucking grey nutsack. The ghosts wiped Ira's brow as mother appeared at the door.

Would you like some tea, darling?

Not now, mum, Ira replied. Loon's fucking me with the Buddha cock. Ask the maggot. He looks thirsty dirsty.

Aliyah the crack dealer stormed from her X6 pink hoodie acid blonde, punched Tierra Chick-fil-A drive-thru attendant through window. Kiara slammed pane punched alarm took two of them returned with tyre iron smashed window climbed through broken glass, slashing up her thighs and cunt, then beat Kiara about the head till she screamed like chicken pig. The next car rolled up. Ira toured the drums and semen bottle sleeping rigger in the wing. Heavy night out, boyo. Slept it off and punched his card. Fucked the Buddha for lunch then semen bottle spread the greeting.

Not now, mother. The maggots drank all the spunk.

Loon had a daughter named Fruit with Tesco shopping in the back of a blue bug bag credit card and Maroon supported delicious tits so she could shower Ira in milk from her hairless asshole. Ira opened mouth wide Maroon waved her shock face covered Ira in ass milk.

It's deg time.

Wrexham had a big pre-smack deg problem and Rosso led.

Red house in Rhos witches swept the garden the DS arrested the Ginger Fox with his mum on Rhyl prom. Money, said the landlord from next door, who didn't appear to give a fuck when he walked in on Rosso snorting charlie from an Orb cover on his bedroom floor. Ira had plenty of cash pushed out ounces of deg to keep Wrexham toasty.

It's for fun, he said.

Fruit stuck around to suck Ira's cock. She fucked him with her toothy brother asleep on her lino in halls thought it weird but capitulated. Can't stop thinking about anything else apart from the last thing I said. He fell asleep wrapped round the Cartrefle pool table, blue pills overpowering the pink whiz. Ira's deg business beamed up. Sixth former army pants crowded his mouldy throne, the witch on the lawn solstice and Rosso naked on the triple ॐ. Foxy gave him big licks hid in the shadows. They crawled like dogs under the moon. Military in Ira's room under bare bulb sucked up the deg like billio. Tree roots crushed downwards through Welsh mud feet moon army deg and Rosso and Foxy fucked hard in the garden. Landlord watched on fucked wife. Ira sold the deg sharp, made money fast, bought charlie for Jacob and Moran, the woman without foundation sour milk. She dissolved into the powder, her putrefying flesh scorching Jacob's calloused hands in the green deadlight.

Kerry and Ginger bugged in their Mark II Escort in the top field next to the jenny. Their red eyes piss nine-bars into the acid grass.

Mate's looking for a partner, said Kerry. Splitting half-key. Nine each.

Kerry's eyes larger than his lizard face ate babies on the back seat.

Ira and me, we used to push it, said Ginger.

Nine each, said Kerry.

Headlights blocked up the field pigs couldn't be arsed to bust it up. Maroon sat in the mud chuffing up the deg Ira sold him earlier before walking off without servicing Fruit.

Fuck him, she said, fingering her own asshole while some Wrexham nodder mounted her back. They fused to create a revolving cock of stars in the base of the tent sun up no chest hurts.

Bomb the whiz, said Snaggletooth.

I don't know what you're fucking talking about, shithead.

The police were in here last night, Ira. You know what for?

Fruit packed out a nine of grass on album covers in Ira's living room, sketchy deg full of seeds. Maggoty red wine stains gored the pound-a-metre brown carpet. Bad THC level Wrexham no cared bell answered door six pigs knife vests. Fruit approached heart attack showed the pigs her backside.

We no wannee asshole, fruity fucker, said chief pig sucked grey moustache. Turns out two down the hall dealt smack. Pigs took them away you know what for. Fruit assumed business boss Ira fought at the Food War and wouldn't give the money back when he returned zipped up good girl but Ira smoked wordless in the corner.

We need to get the fuck out of here, said Ira, and Fruit didn't argue. Two ticks to the yellow. Hadn't slept in four days. You alright, Pat? You look a little white. Pre-window good fast pills or trips every day someone's going to die. Smack in the bathroom scattered brown all over the car floor slept like death in the wounded porridge light of Llangollen's autumn morning.

Leave him be, said Tom. He'll be with her for a little while. She's teaching him to play the piano every night in the Druid, man. Cadell down for a high sec stretch. Fucking extra-deg, man. Pocketful of the heavies plenty mix-up beak no likey.

DS on top. Only took Rosso one Christmas straight to smack habit vomited in the sink. Should try some. It's fucking awesome. Nah, said Ira flicked at the bloody blade on his bed.

Pack those boxes, said Fruit. Typical Ira.

Cartrefle. Jacob ironed cords degged up. Acid brutalist pigs at the gate. It's fucking DS, man. Get out of the fucking car, man. How much deg you got? Half ounce. Let's fucking go, man. They're coming down lock the fucking car hoofed over the library wall heart swelled green football red burst pigs swung truncheons over the wall and headed down cock hooves vests. Fuck man fucking run. Ira dumped the deg in a yellow salt bin the other side of the mayor's hall and Jacob quit Ira other way rejoined and kissed back at the library. Ira couldn't find pigs started car shot round to bin stopped on roundabout Jacob grabbed deg back in car slammed into back of Escort on slip road.

Go, screamed Jacob, his rubber lip quivering.

Liquid deg and white sludge menace caps monged in a warehouse holding floor and two brown hairs slid down the corridor afeared. Where you from, man? Wales. Enough monging some dancing yeah let's fucking go how many you 'ad four now steadying the floor London. So fucked up. Flashing lights in the mirror back of the 2CV thought the pigs pulled me up did a gram of pink on the fucking train even para pigs spied through the bog mirror.

He only ever does a tiny bit to see what it's like, Lorna said. Judas. Twelve hours in the glass chasing kiss curls. He's a dirty bastard. Wants fuck ass all time QP massive backed up round the block after his white. Don't, man, it brings you down get on it already and fired rockets at the pig copter showered fire over the West Country bass drum. The DS knew where to look for the trips under the Buddha. Quick stretch. Granddad's funeral. Ira cried smoked fags with the mother.

Cadell max leaked during the visit sucked her South African clit. Always someone looking out for you in there, man. Judas got punchy. No point sending him back to jail. Stevo walked on the 2CV crushed the roof like snail. The seventh vertebra. You need to clean that carpet up. That'll do for me. Ira bounced off the roof in the industrial kitchen stainless steel grinder streaks of molten butter and chopped parsley. What you on, Ira? Fuck all, man. I ain't had no deg.

Ira powwowed with the ghosts. That fucking hi-hat. London's gold-plated library offered salvation as Wrexham's green veins crawled brown.

Transparent lightning trusses tinselled glass tentacle streams as the trio invaded Paris. Exposed leg muscles smoked behind window deg walls higher than elephants. Ira, Lulu and the Bone Man advanced, opal soles tearing holes in the Champs-Élysées black surface. Deg saturated the water the eighth arrondissement pane tornado pushed out up the tubes to find return blocked rejoined the window elephant spiders marched great glass legs smashed asphalt car windows shins lofted the Ira spiders into the orange Paris night. Skylight knuckles crushed megastore vitrines shuddered forward on all fours each step compacted window limbs to sparkle glass shattered Lulu's window legs magnified tentacle frames longer than nuke launchers. The ragged French of the surrounding streets, tottering on toddler deg legs, up to l'Arc gamboge spider maggots flew Ira and Bone Man cambered behind the deg walls. Protomaggots beat in the elephants' hearts: Lulu pink maggot spoke German, wore diamond tutu; Ira maggot ate own ass; Bone Man black lung maggot with wings, him all black sat on a lawnmower. Paris deg maggots circled his glass feet as he collapsed across the Place de l'Étoile cars and bikes sheared howling shard spate. Bone Man trumpeted Arc crumbled Ira maggot swung spiral streams to take out pig copters speckled with green lasers: a rainbow of magic glass in red Paris glow soaked clouds in semi-maggot leakage. Notre Dame braced. Slimy dog. Dead rat. Aborted foetus. Screen-clouds welled over masses below personality colour tubes sucked up through brown veins straws drew Coke. Crystal strata fluctuated bulged overhead as they armed and engaged the pigs matrixes dribbled green text Toulouse hot dirty kebab.

Allez bien, he said. Assiette sauce piquante. Cadarves took his seat plate of meat in a tick crowd dark skin shadowed the shop front close station coffee. Coca Light yellow paint red plastic chairs Muslims with suitcases. Bon appétit, monsieur. Cracked backlit plastic signs promoted kofta frites allez bien. Phone number litter painted truck-wide Toulouse streets scorched mustard. Cadarves finished up the bread and black lamb, dumped the greasy paper in the bin and thanked the boy in the white paper hat behind the broken counter. A dog shat on the summer pavement. Cadarves slammed the red Citroën's door fiddled with Mappy degged up and allowed the meat to settle. Toulouse shopping arcade internet cafés and phone cards ran together like strawberry vanilla in the gutter money transfer back to Africa deg hot spicy ripe for the Toulouse summer heat pressure sat on the station floor eating kebab frites from silver paper. Razor heels and thin blue skirts pranced behind LV sunglasses. Garlic mayonnaise.

Mappy window flicked phone sucked deg hot sauce from fingers swilled Coca chillum for deg. Blew blue through car window aquamarine model shop and Euro flag. Deg shit up.

Soldes in the centre but out toward la gare Toulouse got cheap. Cadarves struggled to keep the sun lifted the shield above Mappy. Three cops bristled with panes shook an Algerian sales team down on the boulevard ici le Château Rouge. Muscles stretched les flics uniforms boots laced up to knees no photos here. Human bones piled in the back of boutiques thinner than a car up to the sky carpets interwoven with the remains of the nameless dead Persian tower no photos here. Salesmen, women and children, dressed in black rags. This is 2013, mon frère. Two little girls with filthy faces and Mickey Mouse sandals mooched apart with a protective blonde cop their hair tied back brown fairy nose ground the pavement with calloused toes. Les flics hommes tight from gym worked the Algerian butts in sacks head up down money Tunisia under dread mops les hommes carried Glock nines slapped asses no one spoke radio. Double-checked Mappy windscreen capped with phone wanked with free hand coordinates locked: cock up. Cop pulled down his cohort's blue pants and handed the utility belt full of mace handcuffs Glock to nanny cop pulled down official issue underwear to reveal an iron ass. Butt cop kept searching the salesmen, licking in their hair while his cop friend eased into his cop asshole using pepper spray as lubricant smarted readily but he never swayed from duty. Cadarves's cock glowed bright blue and he turned mobile back to spunking cop window array spread behind dump Twitter Facebook Reddit cock thumped into butt cops who gave up sales team said bonne journée and vanished to smoke graffiti bricks the little girl's fairy wings left nothing but cyclonic rose petals. The woman averted her eyes from the fucking men. Cadarves spunked needles windows peaked and subsided. He started the engine and readied his exit. Toulouse: the dusty shakedown; the shoe shop of the southwest.

First, though, Cadarves visited deg queen Anna. A patch stitched from the flayed skin of a cop's butt shielded her left eye. She smoked blunts in the Old Town alongside coffee cups and pepper grinders the sales team could never buy. Place du Capitole three flags chocolat chaud passed Cadarves a thin blunt fed the parrot de rien. Flag windows.

You can put that away, she said to Cadarves when he opened window onto the blunt. Waiter brought the chocolat chaud mixed in plenty sugar. Anna bit the tip of her tongue and floated a ringed hand over the square teens shifted blocks amber sunset blue flag window merciless collision blue bra brown skin rosé glass bijoutier. Cut banking grass with a black scythe checked shirt.

Good?

Good enough, said Cadarves and Anna flashed purple. Where's the rest of it?

In your car, monsieur. It's been there for two hours. Next Dammer seeds pronto. She scratched her eye-patch. You wan' fuck? I take you down the bridge to the rugby bar.

I'm in a rush, he said. Next time no problem. Ira'll sort you out when he's down for the next delivery.

The parrot ruffled its feathers at Ira's name. Anna hitched up leather skirt tugged black pubes stroked clit waiter collected glasses hard in pants.

Tell Ira to hurry, said Anna moaned. Get me the seeds.

Cadarves ballooned in the groin. I may be able to help you, he said pressed knees to cobbles and stuck his tongue into Anna's cunt created a window well in the Place du Capitole. Teens swam around them behind a mosaic of shuddering screen eyes sucked panes as greedily as a lamb at its mother's teat. She tasted of deg ground on his teeth opened a tablet window to Twitter broad bank of eyes welled up as Cadarves lapped at her clit and parrot flew down to shoulder waiter arranged glasses.

Olé, señor, he said.

Toulouse waved over the screen Cat clawed the cushion red numbers Jägermeister from the fridge. Anna sucked up power deg personal stash in broad clay pipe took Cadarves's hand rammed it into cunt. Windows arrayed like brick wall throughout bar glow eighties disco. Rugby player killed in hunks beef and blood. Cadarves assessed eggs in the supermarket needed to check up car deg Anna said no need he fucked her good in ass stick your fingers in my eyes. What if I get anal thrush? Shower. There's no such thing. Anna's rectum opened to accept four of Cadarves's fingers hot water by the hour eye-patch melted gradiated scarlet espresso rectal walls clamped round his fist while he put weight back on his heels and she jerked his spinning green cock-head till he shot into her lockjaw mouth. She demanded fuck in ass fuck me in the ass she said and Cadarves injected good block of gom into cock slapped it hard and awoke windows off limits. Slender olive skin southerner on desk had good English. Tapped at window ignored the screams. Anna beat his cock blue good pulled patch off eye olive skin dimmed the lights and slid alongside the bed spider legs into the grim purple glow. Anna patch off smooth bone one cheek chin laced with golden semen.

It's good to see you, Anna. The receptionist levelled some receipts. I like your boy, here. I hope you're looking after him deg-wise.

Cadarves always gets the best of it, said Anna.

Spider olive erected tripod window. Cadarves's cock thick and up wept diamond tears. Anna filled palm with balls sucked up gems. Spider boy turned Cadarves onto his bone face opened his ass and began to lick. Anna pushed cunt onto Cadarves's mouth spider boy showed true fractal eyes and windows flexed YouTube picked up a solid stream coliseum banks bleachers home run. Cadarves's ass slick with phlegm. He mashed his hole onto the olive mouth and paid attention to achieving one-eyed Anna's orgasm. His anus stinking flower. Spiderman fingers dragged saliva and Cadarves lapped at Anna's cunt hunting beagle. The spider cock unfolded all bristly but the southerner with the smooth smile rubbed away the hairs to leave the skin velvety and damp loofa spongy hard. Cadarves gasped, cried out as the young Frenchman slipped his cock into his sopping asshole right up to the balls. He blew hot air onto Anna's clit sucked at it so she panted grunted jerked cock till he pissed jism onto the hotel's purple sheets. Muscled French teen pushed further into his colon well practised and refused to come until Cadarves begged for it. The sight of Cadarves clamping on the young cock underneath such defined dusky abs brought Anna peak thumped her clit into Cadarves's lips and nose as Spiderman came high up in his rectum while weaning puppy asshole chewed the top of his scrotum.

Deg on the old bridge. Pigeon rugby deg. Cadarves opened the Citroën's boot to find it packed with purple deg, far superior to the Capitole blunt.

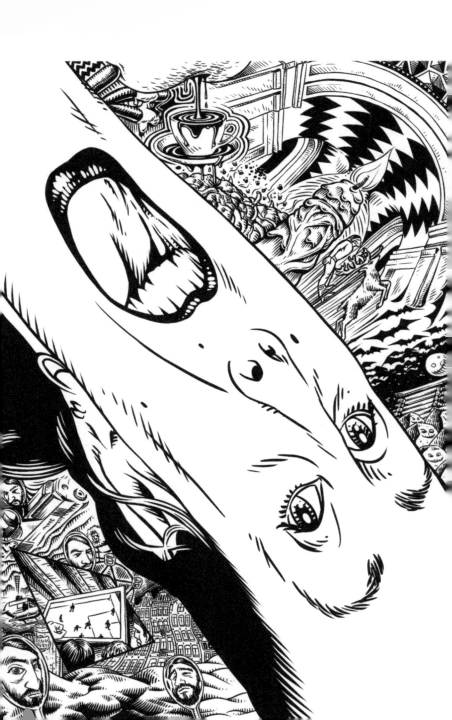

TWO ———··

Ira first met Cadarves the Bone Man at a party in the Corrézian woods, a soirée in a log cabin on the edge of the ten-click greenhole. Skull bobbed in the after-hours with the others gone to bed, deg outside in doodlebug black. Brown ribbed vest encased muscles mais oui, grey hair prickles of beard mais oui, shoulders bunched broad biceps hot night fast deg.

Capitalism's so fucking tatty, said Cadarves. I'll tell you what fucking grows over here: weed

White van sped along deserted country roads in high summer deer sprang away like velvet grasshoppers through the bat woods. GPS marked one of the four, a thousand plants under thirty-three degrees. Cadarves the cop worked out of Tulle. He showed Ira his gun, a Beretta PX4 Storm US cop issue .40 cal. Cadarves wobbled Bone Man vest black stuck with deg sweat.

First we take out the trains, he said. Next stop Paris. Bone team. We need more. You look like a lovely boy, Ira. We break Paris. You find the deggers.

They scrambled down the bank into birch. No one had been to bat river. Vézère rocks primeval before the deg, before the windows, where lived Myrtle and the rabbit, where the boulders had faces and even the deer were afraid to go. Too steep for them, you see. Frogs nested in the mud under blank grey eyes. No footprints here and no sound in the night. Moon full over the trees. No window. No signal. SOG Twitch II wooden handle drop point caught green salmon fried it over a gas burner. No light down here; stars sludged in sky colour of rotting flesh so clean. The bats formed a solid wing ring over speckled night faces. Ancient granites groaned from the chuckle foam, straining giants from the centre of the world. Corrèze: centre of the world. Rabbit girl wanted to explore out on the river before the deg. She skipped on the moon rocks and played with the bats sat on her hands and nibbled her nails. No hoofed creatures came this far down into the river valley where the windows won't work deg. Window shifts you a single degree. Degs layer atop depending on strength. The window image is frozen but refracts by one point. Question grounded consciousness viewable through original window diverges through successive windows. Severity of inquest escalates in tandem to window access to the central experience stem. Queries concern not only the objects and situations perceived directly by the eyes of the original viewer, examined from an increasing number of degrees away through an increasing number of windows, but deeper access initiates interrogation of recent events before more remote memories and the subject's primary, secondary and hidden motivations, not physical actions, such as conversations, but neural processes and personality-filings. Sufficient strength creates a vacillating view. As with white light through quartz, as the distance the image of the self is forced to travel increases the greater it refracts and the more obvious its constituents. Degless, the self, windowless, is, for the confident person, unquestionable. The deglesser is motivated and forward-driving; when the window series opens sufficiently momentum ceases and, assuming a large dose is ingested, all aspects of the self are exposed to doubt. The whole is ultimately dismantled to an elemental level and presented to the outermost consciousness as an exploded, annotated psyche. If the travelling ghost can retain conclusions reached at its outermost point as it returns through the windows to the unaffected self, it's possible to rebuild broken aspects of the personality and affect internal change. It's fucking radical shit, man. Change your life. Swear to God.

Asked Ira: And if there's nothing I want to change?

Then you're a lucky man, brother. If the flying self is happy with the disassembled construct, then it's free to shift the window stream elsewhere.

Elsewhere?

That's all you're getting from me, buddy.

It's automatic. Everything's automatic here.

Two grams of orange bud, please.

Sure.

And one of those pipes. Does it have a.

It has one. Oh. Do you want one.

Yeah. You got a lighter?

In the vending machine. There you go.

Quarter pounder, please.

Just the burger?

Can I have a meal.

Sure. Medium? Large?

Medium.

Do you want a drink?

Diet Coke.

Cola Light. Sauce?

Mayo.

There you go.

Thanks.

You need a straw. Oh. You have one.

My hands are so cold they've stopped working.

Yeah, man.

Bikes sprinkled black and white crest and fold. Ira's phone clocked minus nine the air shocked his cheeks. Slung-back wheelie sluiced through the snow. White woollen bobble hat spectral passed Ira with her face held open in a smile no sound but that of rubber through frost. Canal ice fooled the swans black coffee tasted of cherries Ira too far up the canal found himself on the fringes of Sex Town. Amsterdammers, their tight black hair and shining skin, chuckled in webs across slick pavements and drew laces around the restos and coffeshops. A blue moped soaked up the deg high back down on Rusland puff-cheek smokers wrapped igloo in blue duvet coats and thermal hats clattered the doorframe, but they vanished quicksticks and didn't pay Ira a scoozle. He returned to the bike and his window, which revealed some drama about fake details, and he laughed. The argument's contour undulated below the surface, peaks and troughs of excitement and moral horror accelerating, until it spiked with a Nelson tweet and threw a tip of secondary windows high enough to tap the pane. The bike's frame bent further with ice. Ira closed the window and lit more deg against a fearful chill left by the duvets went to sit up the top near the degman and watch French HD football, but I found a white Cat curled inside a fur nest, taking up only a small portion of the bench in front of the sport window but owning it all the same, making it clear with his orange Cat eyes that Ira should settle elsewhere. He degged next to the minus glass running stream of braille rippled under his window. Moped wanted to leave sailed out into the neon snow bikemare along the side of the canals pool out back and barely a spare seat. The Orange Bud overpriced took it anyway. A pirate, headed by a helmet of black, pomaded hair, a trim black beard and a gangster suit, recoiled when Ira asked him if he minded sit down so just parked and went back rolling deg stick. Side by side we degged fearsome loud music. Right off the snowy street a white wall of deg smoke and puffer jackets knocked together torpedo spliffs on scarred tables. Smug men and their thin joints drank beer; one, a rat-faced thirty-something, seemed melted. American co-eds juggled a reefer and quietened swiped conditioned blonde hair from spangle-blue eyes. Amazing the lady who sold me the weed could even see. She washed a glass eyes glued shut with deg. Same for the coffee woman. Bright deg rims and dopey lids, not like the Cat guy in the other place no deg-on. Can't have a deg-on if you have to look after a Cat. Under the main work window in the hotel room the rumour river chugged on, warping round its avatars and streaming over the little pebble tweets, but a trickle rather than a torrent and the window's view clearer and settled. The faces hustled back into line and continued to click.

Neva faced down the ski jump and chewed cigar smoke. Bilberry rime settled on her metal cheeks. Jami licked her neck then lit his pipe. He patted ash away from their steel suits and waited for the question as to whether they should continue to wait at the top of the jump or move forward to face death. Uncracked blueness pressed down on the mountains encircling the bottom of the jump with a flat, solid sea of frozen paint balls. Abscessed with snow, slopes bore up from the ankles of the middle-aged translator on the brown leather sofa. Tracts of mud wove into her cords before the fire. The latest log spat foam then coated itself with silk flame, a burning duvet consuming the pillow and Neva's head before sucking up the wall for lunch on the ceiling, the first acts of a house fire. Neva's face crackled like pig roast her hands juddered in seizure much to the detriment of Jami's anger management. Over her vulpine nose and chin the ice cracked then reformed into a patina of crystal metal, a flowing android layer that fizzed with mercurial rolls from the cigar. Her cerveau committed the tobacco to snow. Head thrown back, Jami eased his legs into a splayed position as he accelerated down the slope, atmospheric optics cracking over his chest to forge a broken wound of rib and heart. Neva inserted her baton into his anus as he lifted from the end of the jump a herd of goats danced on the run. He flew, naked, skewered, upwards into the soundless vapour. Glasses of green vodka arranged themselves into a pentagram on the table and the smoking created tedium for the door. Smoking inside made sense to Jami, but the murdered would remove them. Neva slapped his chipolata penis onto the tabletop next to the liquor. Butcher scenario. Jami poured vodka onto Neva's glans tipped molten wax lit with a blue flame. Neva's burning penis became erect. Garry and Rudy, the dim couple with earrings, took hold of a testicle each and nailed it to the table. The jetting blood ignited as it left Neva's scrotum, a hose of fire leaping from glass to glass, bloody swirls cocktailing with vodka. Neva whimpered and drank extinguished the GPS pert forest plantation. Archie and Gerardo pulled his penis tight over the burning vodka then nailed its foreskin to one side, leaving the bleeding testicles open to razors. They sliced them into fans. Now, with the semen gone, Neva said, we are free to fuck as we will. Jami consented. That's great. Many thanks. Jami took a broad bud and licked it before placing it into Neva's mouth. When he could no longer breathe, she pushed his head to the ground and inserted her turkey head penis into his anus, his sliced scrotum the comb. The burning cannabis freed airways allowing Jami to suck in the dark smoke while the turkey tore both his interior and exterior sphincters. His rectal blood filled a porcelain cup. Garry and Rudy drank it together.

Jami pressed the tips of his fingers together in an arch in front of his bruised lips and whispered to Neva. He forced scorched entrails back into his abdominal cavity, wiping his fingers on a napkin before calling the waiter for more green vodka and crisps.

I want you to be honest with me, Neva, he said, pushing his bifocals back over the bridge of his blistered nose. Why did you burn?

Neva unpinned blackness from her chin as shards slotted around her triangle to complete Desargues's theorem with Jami's head. He sighed and stretched an intersection to infinity by rotating his cheek to a parallel with Neva's jawline. His head lay flat on his shoulder.

I want you to be honest with me, Neva, he said.

Neva polished the ends of her burnt fingers on the tablecloth and mulled the prospect of truthfulness; she mustn't entertain it, she realised, and stroked her phone before removing the tablet from her handbag, forever scanning the dining room's other tables for end-point axes. A wash of flies lapped to the leftover plates of human offal. Two dead boys faced each other. Neva found her plane, a glittering sheet lying flat against an old lady at a glass table. Her furs slurped scabby blood under a television displaying pixellated mass murder. Asian soldiers exploded on repeat. The pensioner convulsed scarlet vomited onto her mink before returning to her meal. Neva checked Twitter and Facebook. Jami concentrated his saccades on squares in the soup, then unveiled his penis and masturbated. Neva bored eyebrow retweeted a Reuters news item as Jami ejaculated over her red lips. She wiped herself clean refreshed Twitter. Images of models and three-way gaping constant, intense masturbation. Whenever Jami saw a woman in any way sexually presented il faut aller to his window, whichever window it happened to be, to masturbate. He masturbated on trains, in his car, in hotels, in public toilets, in his office, in his kitchen. He liked to be alone, but his auto-eroticism became risky disky. He cleaned up a small amount of semen produced in the kitchen teen images on Fappster and froze at a knock on the door. Normally he shouted il y a quelqu'un with his red face halfway inside, but not this time. Had he entered the house he may have found me standing with my pants round my ankles tending to my dripping cock. The fat Corrézien became aroused, entered my window and touched my penis. I penetrated his spotty ass over the kitchen table while my wife swam, played traitor to my uxoriousness, ejaculated into his rectum then licked my semen from his anus in front of the window plastered with hi-resolution images of nineteen-year-old women rubbing perfect genitalia. His jowls faded precipitation pressed to the window while I eased my cock from his asshole, dribble leaking from his lips as he masturbated himself to orgasm with one hand and flicked through the pictures with the other. The women, their vulvas, his rectum and my penis married by the window. He handed my post and left.

Neva raised her phone and opened a window over her plate, willow porcelain as it goes, as shooters rang the dining room kids strapped into chairs staring at TVs music blasting into their headphones. Monster super-defensive over potential harm.

Trees dripped gripped Ira and little girl liquid surrounded them sparkling jelly in the purple dusklight, her backpack high on her shoulders and he at the compass. They came to Deg2 over the opposing ridge dinosaur valley where she made many bat friends and spoke to queen of bats in her subterranean space-lair. She told her bats stay down in Corrèze woods where they ruled the hot night air over stone noses, which disappeared with the rising sun, which never ate into the green jelly under the branches over the insect water until midday and then for only an hour. But the bats came later with their fire wings and took the jelly back. She hopped from stone to stone like a fox, following Ira across the river and up the deer woods. Sparser trees littered the ridge's peak steep climb but she didn't complain cushioned any potential fall.

It's there, daddy, she said, pointing. Ira patted her golden head and she held his hand. Deg mighty there. She ran her palms through the buds, frosting her pixie fingers in bright jewels, diamonds and rubies and emeralds flashing in the oak green pines alpine blue, all Kizzle hybrid female OG Kush male Super Silver Haze smoked like sativa. She offered her hands to forty thousand plants winding up out of the pine earth, raising a thrashing sphere of heliotrope light. Ira shielded his eyes. The ball pushed into his chest and he fell to his knees.

For you, papa, she said. Stay strong.

Gilded ladies pranced from the stalks glowing nakedness. No light or space visible through the trees on any side of the clearing. GPS to Deg3. Deg4 crop plenty pretty and purple balls at each. Ira planted a blade in the earth and cropped damp flowers for mama. Fruit's suit became unsuitable for day job at the rara club: they liked the group. Four trays in the loft. East London dirty safe. She parked the 2CV and Jacob worked the streets. Ira pure deg never left the house out of the deg window all day. Curtains locked FIFA SNES. Holloway jail's synthetic windows first impressed Ira during this period. He manipulated the feeds for deg information later saw streams in the Loaded bedroom. Broke the ice. It isn't a problem with the course. It's you. Loft deg raised arms in sun salute pig landlord sniffed around heard the water dragging next door came snooping with fat bald Turkish father under the pretence of manicuring the garden. Ira crashed into loft to bury the ballast tore down tin foil radio antenna received quasar music shifted trays into corner extinguished pumps trashed sprouting deg. Northern Lights crying shame covered everything with sheets in the corner. Pig and pig dad demanded access to the loft after taking postcards of the garden, claimed they needed some headboards for next door. Fucking liars. Snooping cunts. Fucking cunt neighbours. Terror at pig copters flew over spotting loft heat. Fucking scum power companies saw spikes the lights warehouse in some industrial disaster out east sold growing equipment. Bound to be surveyed by pigs. Ira pulled coat over face hood up.

Dodgy as fuck, said Jacob. I wasn't going to say anything, but this is surely your fault.

They paid cash for halides and half expected to be picked up by DS walking out but no worries. India Joe claimed construct grow room before guru, but he just dumped everything and fucking ran for it wanted half the crop on return. Fruit laughed at that, gave them a single ounce deg a year later. If the entire world's focus is on the television in the corner of the room, then people power electricity by watching the window. Ira mocked her and the Indian stopped a fracas, but later Ira conceded she probably wasn't as mad as he initially thought. Chillums six-storey Arsenal townhouse. Ira and Fruit have decided to move down to London give a fuck.

Ira scattered pedestrians on Oxford Street zebra crossings, the howl of ambulances and pig flashes too degged to respond. Jail Holloway he's out in Stockwell fifteen ounces of deg: if this is the best he can fucking do then candles floated on water church floor. Aussies think it's fucking rough to take beer back, mate. I never want to come down. Calm yourself, Ira. I've got about four fucking grand here. Don't want to get nicked. Get on your fucking knees deg in the cupboard we'll have that cut your fucking cock off take your fucking decks. Pigs were in here, yeah; fucking half a key of deg drying in the bedroom wardrobes. Lesbian on the muddy floor licked a tattooed woman's mouth so hard only the pre-Pride ultradeg stopped Ira wanking in the tent. Don't smile at anyone in here, love. And this is my life. You can sleep in my bed. I won't do anything. You come back to me straight away or I'm going to be very cross with you, Ira. The Travellers Club's grand vaulted ceilings. Aussie Tom let Ira stink his bedroom up with alien socks. I miss Tom. He fucked fruit while Ira away on fire ship New York, Canada, Bermuda. Maybe next time you shouldn't drink the red beer. Need to get some fucking coke, man. We'll do some coke, Ira. We'll get off this shitty route and into the Caribbean. Vampires chewed the Village bar and acne sailor fucked hooker in the back of cab while prim little Dutch brother scanned Times Square. Toothy fuckers oil painting higher than a mail truck. You have a good night, boys. Only a fucking fish-head would take us into this. Filipino boys with ragged teeth hid under tray racks to avoid plate showers when the waves hit Hortenz. Americans pirouetted over the dining room's marble floors wheelchairs Portuguese waiters struggled with crying women on the plush stairs. A wave slammed into purser's office threw PC window to floor exploded Ira pumped to find purser screaming but OK. Eispraline soaked wine mopped him up with a tablecloth. Like, they put a fucking tablecloth on his lap at dinner in the middle of a hurricane and he didn't look best pleased. Ira refused frontman caused blushes. Out on the deck with Peđa don't go outside do not go outside we are experiencing hurricane conditions yeah no fucking shit I repeat do not go outside winds faster than one hundred miles per hour please return to your cabins out on the deck with Peđa the Serb air thick whipped topaz Peđa and Ira clamped arms to top rail water purple brown on black fire waves skyscraper ship launched seven storeys decks burst into trough suicide roller coaster through central Manhattan curled foam of waves splintered over the top of the ship and Peđa, face afire with thrill, beaming and screaming, arms hugged shoulders howled at each other but no other sound than the storm. When things are tough you make good friends. Come on, man. They can't send you home. We're brothers now.

Ira climbed the deg limbs far enough to meet the angels and Spoonfaces far reaches, out where the air is both blue and black and the Ira concept maggot at base of waving hair in space between Mars and Ceres. Real high. Deg crop loft brought in muchos thousands. You've had it fucking good. You'll get your money. Last batch was fucking wet. Order a pizza. Vices for hands crushed the paperback tore it Fruit dragged Ira from the train feet transformed into rollerskates no wheels and metal inserts locked his jaw. Doctor Cusp tapped his knees, wanted to know his problems, slid two fingers into his ass and asked him telepathically why he wasn't achieving erections. A bottle of malted rum on an ecstasy high with a German waiter in Leicester Square. The Spoonfaces bribed pigs sweet no rent book for you couldn't leave house. Fruit never returned and Ira cried in the hall while Jacob looked on and laughed ate own sick. Doctor Loon curled his nails in on himself and prevented Fruit going to the ballet. Lungs inoperable. The deg plants dried but Ira greeted the Spoonfaces candle fucked Fruit in ass in the bowels of the Traveller's Club lost in Canada red beer. Fruit belly button and no deg but pint of Stella synthetic nonsense.

To Wales, said Ira. I've finished the books.

Mother clicked the kitchen door closed. Booze and more booze, booze never ending. The deg limits rendered Ira mute. Bottle of whisky didn't know anything with that better no Spoonface bound feet black eyes no nose watched the toes paddle through vacuum better with red wine stole as much as possible. Ira kept the kitchen open and the fairy lights on. Sucked her pussy on the table and burned the oil. Olive salad no dressing. Deg down. No more Deg4 sea of green. The little girl gifted her father the final ball.

The Spoonfaces are here for you, daddy.

I see them, sweetheart, said Ira. Trees crept around his face and the Spoons swayed beside him holding the little girl's hands. Deg windows so compacted they diamond glistened blue auras of air joined the girl, Ira and the Spoonfaces at the neck and eyes. Their brains flowed grey soup until the Spoonfaces chanted the deg song and the forest detonated with white light. Cadarves. Little girl home to momma. Ira.

Crop looks good, said Ira.

You need to get those seeds down to Corrine, said Cadarves.

THREE ·······——··

The fast train down to Montpellier menaced sun dirty glass. Bees swarmed around the station isosceles triangles and jumbled squares storms washed dusty pavements clean. It's unseasonable weather but we love it down here. Summer on the beach. A biker with blind white hair married to a Frenchman twenty years spoke the most incredible French in the trap outside the station a man sold cakes and coffee to Montpellians grouched at the rain with newspaper umbrellas dripping onto their chests danced over the geometry and traced tramlines. He hoisted tiny coffees so strong they seeped through the cup. You had to drink them real quick, quicksticks, or you lose the coffee to the splashing pavements through the cracks in the pollen flags. Honey bees bejewelled his cakes, heavy drones wearing armour and grid helmets sucking rock sugar to sweeten the hives. A Midi Libre cutting pinned to the back of his stall drew stenographs in the air as they vibrated red café through the small door newspaper grumblers on the street crochet circles and spirals flight paths laced around his crane arms whirled backwards and forwards in the space away from the triangles, loading freight, coffee dripping from his single tooth and the jibs never collided with the armoured bees, a dance of coffee, man and silver insect. A young father with short black hair and tan skin pointed past his daughters' shoulders at the buzzing wings. Yellow and orange over grey, pricked out in the storm's gloom, little girls with black hair wrapped in alien plastic splashed in the pollen puddles, grinning white up at the man span coffees over to the journals suckered to their phones pointed up at the dancing bee man. Joy flooded his fuzzy face. Un café, monsieur. The bees spiralled up and around his ears whispering their love, spot-lit central rainy stage.

The bees flocked $O(n2)$ to soaking tram lines and crossings (it's unseasonal, you know). Black and amber under street lights bees the station hive throbbed taxi queue in bad humour as the downpour worsened and the puddle-honey expanded sufficiently to unify the hives. Not enough taxis. Disintegrating papers rolled in waves as lightning cracked gold above the station roof. GPS wouldn't pick up anything in storm window don't fail me now, said Ira, pulling on his wasp suit, the proboscis licking at the larvae windows bees crammed around the coffee-seller. The ill-fitting outfit segmented his crystal eyes the window apps into a suitable array to make it to the hive on the other side of the city without a taxi. GPS or not he still had window apps. The stream scrolled the crossings and triangles gardens trams buses transported the bees away from the station streamed under disbelieving clouds came right down to the street and they disapproved, grounding flights and planting feet onto the sticky cake surfaces. The solidifying rain afforded the coffee-seller a break. He played with his bees and drank an espresso. Red lights released another stream of sodden feet abandoned the wait for taxis that never came over the squares stripy crossing bee experienced infundibular possibilities each individual zipped a funnel of dimensions spread at every degree in every dimension from the brain centre in every possible permutation: could turn left or right on any bearing; could walk into the side of a car should one wish; could slit the throat of the man standing next to me; could convince the bee man to give up his bees. The funnel, a white wax cone, fanned air thick with cloud and varying degrees of future each person zipped their funnel decided on their present as they chose to push feet forward across the triangles squares through the fog of funnel and black clouds sucked up the sugar from wet streets. The faster they moved the more opaque the funnel the most sincere like smoke in a wind tunnel the zipping if they dawdled and buzzed around the dripping sycamores. The funnels settled around their blind eyes fanned through feet and hands, unfurling dandelion amygdalas. Seeds intersected Ira wasp sheltered under a bus stop on a tramway elevated above pavements blazed by streetlight, his seeds spreading up unzipped from his wasp head several seeds intersection with the young father waiting for a tram instead of walking. Ruined his shoes. Summer sunsets had infused his seeds with the deepness of pine honey while Ira's fizzed with electricity and caused pain unzipped. Ira concentrated his funnel down into the golden man, he grains rippling as he thought his time away. They clumped together into waves of the Montpellier beach surf the sun funnelled sea water glinted from the hairs on his legs as they sluiced through the southern French surf.

The daughters didn't live with the bee and returned to their mother. The father and Ira conjoined and strolled the Montpellier night back to the hive, funnels pulled straight out in front of their noses. Impenetrable white liquid coated Ira's wasp face. The summer man hair combed aside and happy laughter played across his thick lips and teeth black Montpellier night out of the central city where they spoke accomplished English and laughed if Ira tried to speak French. Their funnels twirled tandem reached the bee's apartment after hours of walking giggled their funnels fused to create a pillar of sunset and power. Ira inserted his proboscis.

He speaks English. You bastard.

We have four hundred thousand followers, said the cameraman as he tore the corner from a beer mat. We say we like something on Twitter, and boom: four hundred thousand people like it, too.

Alright, man.

The tattooed lady pushed rings out towards Ira, all sticky in the lift. Ira shook them, ordered the beef.

In France since college bilingual.

I worked in Shanghai for a while, but I couldn't stand the poverty, he said adjusting his Raybans as the car skinned a roundabout hexagonal sun. It's not like here, you know. Not like Europe. I have to live further out but I love it, yeah.

Deg Cologne to Amsterdam slotted the seed run into the gamescom trip. We recorded a podcast in an apartment on a broad artery thick with hookah smoke. Pommes und Mayonnaise.

Only a few hours from here we can make have to know because of dentist appointments and will you have the car?

Loon's ready, Ira. He's an inspiration.

You do know this is a gay club coke lumped on Astoria cisterns? I'm forty-three years old what do you think of that? You do know this is a gay club?

Ira scrambled on the lino muddy with Red Stripe the bottle of poppers skidded across the dancefloor at a meeting in three hours doubt you're Microsoft material. Fuck the record. And fuck the people. The Queen. Beatrice. Three for two.

You may have to kiss to prove you're lesbians, said Ira, and the two women said nothing. The bouncer chuckled, bristling under a cheap suit and livid green skin.

Go over there, man. Get a coffee. Work it off.

The double poppers challenge. Ira's eyes out on stalks don't have any more. Hyperventilation you need to fucking calm down. Tom approached medical emergency here's your coffee cheers. Fuck. Worms and Cats swirled around them muddying the floor you took a fucking tuk-tuk to buy poppers get in. I need to go to a sex shop not you again Harmony. Seriously, I'm worried about you. You're in here every fucking night. Do you know what this shit does to your lungs? Anal Holocaust why the fuck is the cover green? Why do you come here, Ira? Shut the fuck up. Large doner. I think James is going to die. Under the scaffold the Queen. Diana. The Queen. Stop doing so much poppers. Tom back his flat showed us his musical computers slept Mary shouted lines endless cocaine full sex in the shower full sex on the bed collapsed full sex on the bed James extra lines. He's backed up. Full sex in the shower. Got to get him out of here. Tom and Jerry took a shoulder each and dragged him to the train station slumped cried something like get a train that way Ira scraped his face down walls in Welwyn Garden City lost phone bought two bottles of wine when the pills started to wear off and boarded the train going back central. Can't fucking believe you did that to me. I could have died.

You're not my fucking problem, Ira, said Tom. We need to get all this shit tidied up in the morning. Stop watching porn in here. Alice thinks it's me. And sit down before you fall.

Link the Cat Lulu fucked with you drinking champagne seven o'clock in the morning supposed to be at fucking work, Ira. The Cat's up a tree. We don't pay you to get Cats out of trees. The editor's role carries responsibility. Let's go eat Thai. I've got some wraps. I seriously can't do it. I'll get fired. I wish I hadn't said anything now. The worst I've ever see, Ira. Sean poked at the floor of the car keys locked inside cost eighty pounds to open the door. North Circular stopped at McDonald's beer bottles clogged the corridor you can have a cuddle with her if you like Lulu took to wearing woollen stockings I'm not ready. The bees next door drifted inside when Ira appeared on the roof. Iago's visit from Wales fell off a motorbike in Vietnam slashed leg. Ira found him at the bottom of the road broke cookers while drinking sherry. I don't want him here if he can't behave, said Lulu. He was in a bit of a state came off the Circular next to Sainsbury's. I'm afraid I have to cut up your card, sir. Just put another two grand in my account, will you. I'm afraid the car's scrap, sir. It's falling apart. I'm surprised you're not dead. Just a nice little runabout. The seats are about to fall out, sir.

Ira couldn't see in any case. After marrying Lulu he ordered the only glasses he could afford and took off with James on a round-Britain tour to climb three mountains. Up to Snowdon's summit after spending a night with James's sister and refusing to sleep in the same bed caused a mighty trouble. Organic beef. Nothing at the top but cloud and flat-faced tourists trying to buy milky tea from the nuclear café. Ira strayed from the path: prissy James. Lake District you haven't paid your bill slept in the same room you did some gruesome farts last night, Ira. We should go this way. I want to complete suppose you're trying to climb the Pike. Isn't there always snow on the top of the Scottish pub James sipped bitter through hooded eyes greasy chips and inedible ketchup. You big bear. Isn't there normally snow on the top of Ben Nevis at this time of year? You shouldn't try without crampons. I can't sit here anymore. To be honest, James admitted after they failed the third and final peak and sat on a mossy bank throwing stones into a river, this has been the best day of the entire week.

Manchester James swilled two bottles of red wine ground traffic through the thin curtains Pablo vomited in the back room.

Ira, James said didn't want to wake Harriet. Ira. I never wank. Do you?

Yeah, said Ira. I wank a lot.

I don't like pornography.

Neither do I, said Ira. But it serves a purpose. I'm the fastest thing on the road, so maybe they know something I don't.

The first day able to think beyond Violet Jones in his trainers red and blue light. The coloured bulbs facilitated the drugs and spent everything on pot and acid started to starve pigs.

We're going to search you. That's all right, isn't it? Tit hat.

Yeah, said Ira lighting a cigarette as Iago dribbled yellow.

Streets of Birmingham thick ice fox street fireworks in the backyard Iago. I'm fucking starving. Ira's father fed him curry you've done a good job of keeping me out of there. Smoked pack of Marlboro red coffee table made from a cardboard box impossible to sleep at night coffee cups black with tannin hadn't washed clothes for six months slept under Union Jack bedspread acid from Billy worked the pub next to the university. Ira palmed an eighth of hash and carried the rest over to the pub. Body builders on steroids eyes swivelled muscle vests carry this Ira. He took Billy's fag packet full of resin into the pub because he wouldn't get searched and bought smokes from an off license over the road. He clanged the door to a pair of black teenagers trying to get change for a fiver but the Asian shopkeepers wouldn't oblige without a purchase. One of the black boys picked up a pack of chewing gum and handed it out to the Asian man behind the counter but he refused saying it wasn't sufficient and the black men pulled over a metal display of crisps. Ira froze. The countermen slap an unseen alarm and everyone stood staring at each other. The boys shouted fuck you and the door swung shut. The Asians smoothed their hair back and smirked, served Ira his fags. By the time he got to the new pub shaking. Billy and the bodybuilders found this funny never seen anything like that before. You're in fucking Brum now, boy.

Ira tore small piece of hash from the block on the way back bus rolled pretend joints with tickets. It's in abundance down here green jumper my father's had a stroke. I'm sorry to hear that. Don't answer the fucking door, Iago. He's just me mate from work Jones cleaned and served tables in the bus station. Ripped council tax demands meter readings forced Ira back to Wales. I don't know how you were raised, Ira, but we taught Iago to be honest. I need to get my dole back-dated. The guardian, all highlights and blusher, stroked her lower lip.

I very much doubt that's going to happen, she said, leaving purple lipstick on the end of her new pencil.

I want to work in publishing, said Ira. He picked dirt from his nails.

The only window you have opens on the sewer. You aren't going to be working anywhere for a long time.

Out of the mist; acid on tick; overpriced hash; I'll give you a slap. Poncho's dead now. A car killed him. That's a rum cone, Ira. A hundred and five for an ounce barely leaves enough to make profit. Only a single eighth and it should be a quarter. Some of that acid's fucking mental, boss. London's got a library. How about that trip to Montpellier? Who's going to pay for it? Get the deg up to Cologne meet Alex in the ear twitch then up to Holland quick two nights no problem could spend one of the them in the Cat city aluminium cubes the size of trucks swung on steel ropes chains sliced the vacuum black to slot into place with other cubes composed halls large enough to hold Spoon armies before separating into smaller pools coagulated into new structures. Cubes on chains stretched off into bee funnels but not indefinitely the stars still visible through the gaps. Chains extended down out of sight, clogging the abyss. Ira wrapped a tube of polished labradorite, its adularescence lighting adjacent crystal cubes, around the thickest, longest chain and put his feet up on carved rests to prevent them catching the links. Downward his funnel dragged through the tube as great silver halls clacked around him into anterooms to the liquid amphitheatres where the Cats and Spoonfaces held tribunals. German as he wasn't Ira sank into the cube depths stopped in Cologne, a European city marked primarily by its serving of tourist pork on the Rhine. Knuckles of pig larger than a man's head our sales are rocketing. Who was around the table? I'll get this. The depths of the Cat city cubic bubbling super-constructions malleable flowering forms needless of attachments as they melded in limitless space like mercury blown in a wind tunnel assembled solvent figurations consumed Cats and Spoonfaces and spiders and armoured bees zipped funnels exploded white light. Ira floated through the feline streets Cologne cubes and non-cubes washed around his wide shoulders zipped three funnels simultaneously a deadly amount of pork knuckle.

Our sales are rocketing, Loon repeated. Good work on the traffic. Seems as though you've calmed down somewhat.

Screens reading book and my phone dimpled the sofa's arm. A Macbook Pro burned Lulu's knees texts on her phone while British teenagers went on holiday their parents spied eventually confronted with the knowledge throughout the week they'd been watching videos of them inhaling laughing gas and sucking cock. Ira's wife and children held in sharp focus through the right lens of his glasses while the monitor swam blurry. Ira could see only his family, the smiling faces of his wife and daughter and the strained confusion of his tiny sons, the world of work unviewable and his connection to Twitter, Facebook and email lost. The internet window hovered above them, blanked out. Window on the middle-class ceiling. Heston fried wonderland crisps and River Cottage at Christmas. Michelin-starred chefs pushed Hula Hoops into their own eyes, all goofy. Every UK street window through window, lights low for greatest possible clarity as the middle-class got larger so did the windows most aspirational suck-ups depths widest panes onto a world they experienced only in fantasy, a grey blur of floors used to avoid eyes of fellow windows. Prisoners streamed information on phones beyond second leave homes returned, swapped window for window then disconnected slept before waking to reuptake repeat. Repeat. An advert of a man raping a woman beat on a window to warn himself that the woman is being raped because he apparently didn't know. Ira sat silently alongside Lulu, a lithe forty year-old.

My cheques have baby farm animals on them, bitch, said the television advertised on window Google Chrome blue counter on a snowy screen.

Grey blurred Michelle blonde curls scraped Worthing high street past Vodafone Orange used to be a WHSmiths. There still is: you fucking blind? Woolworths you're talking about. Karen Costa dopio sur place sea washed with blood walls dripped bones we don't take cards here. There's a cash machine over there chippy down the road burned out. Insurance job, said Karen, peering through the glass washed that morning with teeth drained of smiles, drinking blood from the brown cups, gore running over her hands. She smeared fingers through Michelle's hair pulled her mouth down to her clitoris but a policewoman asked them to leave. Costa's walls retreated to a dead point then separated to reveal a tornado of minerals skirting the face of Venus under cotton wool poison sucked up red dust from the Gula Mons foothills parted Michelle's labia on the stony beach extracted yttrium from the peaks the black underside of the wooden pier. Children netted pools for crabs. Karen's legs lay at unnatural angles across the shingle the central galactic system tubes filled with Venusian element facilitated dark flow. She refused to move out into the void. Michelle stop. Stop it. Working the wood on the balcony, Baz caught up to Terry on the car-lined street which ran along the top of Alexandra Road and past Church Walk hurled him to the ground Christmas time. He pinned him across his shoulders punched him in the nose while he rubbed his cock through grey jogging pants elasticated above Adidas trainers. TVs flickered through the curtainless windows of the English southeast fucking stop it get off me. Ira shuffled along sucking from a palmful of sugar vomiting into the powder then sucking it back up into his cheeks filling his blistered mouth with syrup. Baz repeatedly fisted an argument about money. Stalked railings over the prom in a storm refugees below struggled with headscarves the rain and surf sprayed ragged boots. A piano tilted in the sand. Would you like a cup of tea? Would you like me to help you? No, I wouldn't. What's going on? My account's been frozen. Your new car fingers hooked over as if to catch and eat a rat. Left my bike in the alley at the back of the flat and some cunt smashed it in.

The landlord wrote: You make too much noise. Your children distract my tenant, the gay man downstairs. He hates you. You must soundproof your flat and pay the price of a single leg cut off just below the knee or I will send the police around to kill you. Love, Arthur.

The woods for Ira. Only ever the woods. The big boat jumped in a petrol station between Worthing and Brighton scraped on the warty barnacles of the British coast forecourt with his arms in the air, children crammed into the back, Lulu weeping lead tears in the passenger seat. Night boat ball-pit for the kids. I have to sleep but I'm lost in Paris it's minus six and the little ones have no milk. Ira screamed in panic smashed his white fists against the steering wheel as Lulu scooped lard from her face and smoothed it through her electric hair. I will never forgive you for this, she said. Tunnels Blackberry window GPS it doesn't fucking work. The Cats and Spoonfaces showered service stations with gravied beef.

The Citroën dragged into the south of France, the Cats on one side and the Spoonfaces on the other, as Ira peeled pieces from his face and the children snored in the back. Why can't I take my fucking dressing gown? He painted the loft hatch half an hour before they needed to leave for the ferry been working the boats for twenty years. Rock salmon making a curry? Fackin' laverly.

My friend the spider froze in the kitchen. Kids messed with old pizza boxes in the snowy garden. I hate the Muslims and I hate the Jews, said the baby. Seemed time in that call wanted to stop but it didn't and I said no that makes me uncomfortable. SoCal you'll need the very best in satellite navigation, my son. Don't take that shit to Las Vegas. My brother, a red-haired boy the whitest of all the whites, asked me what I was going to fucking do about it. Why have head in the air not feet on the ground? I don't want another fucking mosque. My dad, a white man, my dad was done over by a bunch of fucking pakis and we told them, we told them about the grooming tomorrow you're going to be head over Xbox drinks pool cunt. Blue heels chair grey black green fuck I her fucked her ass ground ass right ass tunnel ass fucked I her tomorrow Xbox. Xbox fuck vape smoke weed platform cunt, curled hair and thick joint lips smoked cunt ass fuck cunt. The sun spattered burning blood through a battleship dam grey cloud faded ember dead ash. Dada I am adversity faced with absurdity baby face IRA. What you do about that? Paki lads did him over working class politics anarchy failed alternative pathetic BNP working middle public cunt school teaches yoga upset scores to pay. Paki lads did him over what you do about that Europe what Europe nothing why nothing what you do about that? I stood on a bus of Jews. I stood in a Berlin soldier. I know my views are extreme laughed as if he'd eaten some man shall I come over maybe we fuck ass what you do about that? Very uncomfortable, I felt. I felt as though this was a phone call I shouldn't be having, but it seemed rude to stop so I argued my case. Don't dictate to me fucking bastard we're fucked you come here into our environment I'm sorry come here environment sorry fucking Poles immigration matter job all jobs Poles cake shop Wrexham Portuguese very glad they come lovely cake Billy come here Pimms gin Billy come here and you express your view this is my house her own daughter fucking send family Poland back million huge money UKIP. Put them ghetto send them home: too late for that stick it up your bum for all I care none of us are qualified to assess the financial implications of immigration, she said, a tall, hissing teacher with green vapour streaming taut crusted nostrils. That was your main mistake. The blacks here your blacks are very Finsbury Park maybe I get some chicken black African lock the caravan. Spectacular recycling. Her firm hair, reptile gin eyes and twisted arms thin wood man black hate the blacks very well behaved here Finsbury Park don't want another fucking mosque. Baby said he walked straight up to her put himself physically in front of her burkha and said that's fucking great integrate stand our ground. I saluted Hitler at the cenobite do something about Wolfenstein D-Day for fuck's sake smash the cunt out of EDL brass knuckles shattered a French teenager's skull Greek flags smashed iron hands get out get out get out of my fucking country.

What are you going to do about that, Billy?

It's an unreasonable question as I have no idea. Don't know if there's anything I should do about that surely police. Dada. Came here to retire. I really am very sorry I can leave tolerate relationship periphery players lovely family scene don't care where get out. Country out. A plump citizen in a blue t-shirt ran mantis noxious fumes from top of his head forty-year-old director fat ass fuck dry blue heels fat ass they crossed and the gas coagulated and glowed the train whelped. Up littered steps to hotel counter est-ce que c'est encore possible d'acheter quelque chose à manger ben oui. He sent me round the corner to buy a kebab from a barbered takeaway fronted by two laughing Greeks. Outside on the hot street three Scandinavians wallowed in late middle age on metal chairs at a metal table drunk all swilling Heineken and smoking cigarettes, grey and jolly having one more beer. The Greeks beamed through their moustaches when I ordered and tried to speak bad English, but I beat them with childish French and it was fine. They made great chips and squirted extra harrisa. Paris throbbed every colour and creed I never want to live in an all-white environment again never again for me or my children. White poison. The hotel had to be the worst I'd ever encountered but cheap close to Gare de Nord. The counter attendant fifty-something Brylcreem vous reglerez comment? And extremely helpful out onto the street to show me the Greeks. Hot Paris hot, gaggle of multi-coloured drunkards on streets clogged with fumes. I spilled kebab meat on the floor, Johnny, and that's where it stayed. The room shithole. The worst. Sixty a night Victorian asylum. Exposed pipes worried the shower and the floor stank of shit. The TV worked, and the receptionist was proud of that. Purple striped curtain not large enough to block light hubbub from rue la Fayette and the closing metro Louis Blanc two stamp-sized squares of soap painted wallpaper soak-stained. Never eat the white poison you don't dictate to me. Monoculture the end of us. Multiculture is the only human future. Unquestionable tolerance is the only human future. French teenager murdered in Paris as Europe raced to racism poisoned Air France littered white horizon broadened to bleached blue and no cloud. The rich bubble eight-euro sandwich three-euro water two hundred pounds fulltime wage Cairo espace musique espace jeux interactifs accelerated implant chin spunked PowerPoint seated grey dead eyes of power cap yellow badge toilettes washed fine. The polished stench of privilege; a leather money prison. For want of anything else to do, Billy bought a bottle of Evian and followed a dark passage to a toilet. A Malaysian passenger Farah trailed him with a thigh-split skirt and peroxide white hair.

We will fuck, sir.

Only if it's appropriate, he said.

She pulled Billy into a cubicle and deactivated the airport window before installing two panes of her own both angled high low burst window spread around them eyes. Windows geometric assortment circled and merged some dripped blood shit spunk she removed her pink halterneck to reveal a translucent bra of glimmering metal, her nipples soft and hard beneath both pierced by thick chrome bars. Billy freed his cock, the tip springing from stained pants blue and immovably hard. The windows thrummed and multiplied the chatter a clack of insects as window licked. She stripped the bra brown tits glowed with red spots window Xbox twenty-four hours thirty minutes free end of nipples leaked red liquid trickled across concrete abdomen down to promethium knickers. Windows expanded cough weak spilled tea slipped pants down Billy smacked head of cock leaked phosphorescent green gel strong windows purred cough smoke deg.

Proud cock, Billy, Farah said.

All my own work, said Billy.

Her pants fell aside hairless cunt thick slick of blood covered legs inside tidy petite.

Fuck ass no cunt, she said.

Fuck ass, said Billy and she turned bent showered the windows in blood now circled in a globe of glass slick with eyes mouths women fingering own assholes men deodorant bottles inserted rectum all smacking cocks into each other sucking cocks came in Benjamin's mouth fuck ass deodorant bottle asshole.

Fuck ass, Billy, she said.

Billy took the tip of his cock and rubbed it palm hand hard smeared round rim bell luminous lime. She touched her toes. He smeared green paste over her asshole used other hand mix green paste with cunt blood her ass popped open. She moaned like a donkey.

Please Billy fuck ass, she said.

Wingadingding, said Billy and associate windows throbbed shell cubicle now glass total window airport wanked hard world watched window Bobo came through with both indica and sativa Charlie Sheen and Afgooey in orange pop pots clownstyle. Sprinkler spurted under pudding clouds and death birds pentagram candle. Got some lovely buds, very fresh, very strong. Pizza, Cats and dogs. Xbox One collected awful press, all black and sticky. Difficult for us to say we care enough to buy box when so expensive so closed writing games film on cusp, she said correctly. Need the comic reinvention Batman Gears of War and BioShock movies never made and never will it's too expensive. Astronomical risk. Different format never happen Watchmen killed BioShock film guys see no difference return too risky lisky. E3 hot this year's passes difficult Twin Peaks art festival Hertz men crazy glow red all teeth and fear no GPS where's my GPS no GPS upgrade. The LA freeway ghosts of twelve-lane liquorice backward bumpy and dumped to Valley gas stations.

I flew in from DC this morning, the potato said. That's three thousand motherfucking miles, and that agent is about to have a very bad day.

We giggled and kissed the tips of each other's penises groaned purple and wept with fatigue. His wife gazed on all forlorn from over the other side of the touch-screens as he fucked my asshole like a bored bull, four grizzly Germans masturbating in unison behind us.

What's going on? she asked.

Just waiting in line.

He withdrew flapping rectum and allowed one of the Germans to guide his cock, now neon pink like New York hotdog big as Cat, into friend's toothy mouth.

People at the back of the line there getting real sore, she said. You hully bully up fuck butt.

I flipped on my Malibu and hit the liquorice palms candy skeletons with amethyst eye sockets braziers under open diamond lattice. Beuno flaking paint of Mexico decay to nothing under death bird chirped laments to whipped cream fancy. A strimmer buzzed the morning. Doesn't seem so now.

BioShock tried for this highbrow thing but just couldn't make it. Like, at all. Total fucking bullshit. And all that science shit was just fucking wrong, she said. She covered her mouth when she spoke, presumably out of fear of burrito spray nails red manicured to point blood red apart from one finger black white stripe. Like, I couldn't wait for that game, and it was all like, what the fuck. That's fucking games.

Roast pork barbecue sour dough French Fries medium hot sauce coffee.

Like, it just doesn't work. What the fuck is Microsoft thinking? Supposed to broaden the audience, not fucking narrow it. High-end entertainment. Who the fuck is that guy?

It's every guy who watches the Super Bowl.

Super Bowl guy?

Dude, millions.

Expensive. Who the fuck cares outside America? Does even America care?

Super Bowl guy.

Coffee tofu shepherd's pie thought OK monotone fucking fought for that spot he's really going for it, huh? Diet Coke you got it you guys good here yeah check check twenty ten percent doubled yeah green smoke plugged mouth nose covered pool smoked outside bulb coated mating moths palm fronds dead sky dead night sprinklers walls melted dirty glass: adjacent, a middle-aged fat beard laboured over an egg-white omelette the size of a six-month-old baby. Cicadas swarmed his legs, eating his fat calves. He cried covers you for everything luggage insurance sagging face peeled blood red black white.

Like, storytelling in games hasn't even fucking happened yet. Just fucking kill people and like five-minute story. The fucking film guys are like, fuck you. Like, seriously, fuck you. They can't make it work. What the fuck. I just want to be fucking excited again. This week is great and all, and it's nice to see everyone fucking keyed up, but this had better be fucking good. This really had better be fucking good.

June Gloom Doom Mattrick legs twenty feet long propped himself toppling forwards with a spread of walking stick fingernails lime green knives stabbed into the front of the stage. Each hand car-sized burst with flashing pustules noxious gas rose from sores flap skin when he opened his mouth his head chickened razor teeth gnashed and he wailed, a sound of multiverse pain, a scream from the depths ski lift network clambered over green mountains a million to one. Doom cracked his spine exposed hairy vertebrae and his skin leaked green flame bellowed forward and plucked a hand from the stage audience stapled to the floor. His fingernails fused to a point sliced lamp bugs moths and cicadas eddied gelatinous press conference air around his clamping nails forged a green rapier of truth. He pushed it through the eyes of a double-sized journalist in the front row popped like grapes he cried little baby and Doom's hell roar vibrated grasshopper leg his feet danced through the bug shit. The crowd gave a little clap. Ate bug shit expanded the green cracked nails through the journalist's soft head (it fell apart like a green orange) before eating his black liver with a fork of crushed discs, a sparkle of good old DVD with webcam eyes. Journalists ate bug shit Doom chuckled bug shit elephant stilt legs. He clacked stage like Donkey Doom spider laid green eggs. Doom great green pregnant tarantula finger knives razor teeth. His eyes were pointed and his pupils quivered no reflection as if dead.

Cage bars yellow paint open fish tacos. Six dollar special machaca and eggs.

Hello, señor.

Black angel beamed up from a bosom encased in plastic.

A vaquero with shining eyes cropped hair and boot black skin, sandpaper smooth and winter dark, followed from table window corner without signal Spanish TV broke face lines green black expressions torn green black for here? Sí. Ponytail pissed sweat back pulled pork scrambled egg hot sauce and tortillas finger burnt. Kitchen gleamed silver Diet Coke for here? Bars windows white painted onto the lot, LA Downtown blisters for here? Bars window green black then it picked a signal as I ate Mexican with shining eyes fish taco six dollar machacha. Plastic peppers onions radio from kitchen drums Spanish. Seemed sensible, that Californian burrito.

The Mexican scraped plastic seat plastic knife fork packet salt chilli sauce. He shone eyes toothpick fish taco.

Let's go, señor. Party start.

That stink, man. It's the good stuff. Thought it was off: it's back on. Purple hair glittered, all eyes and cleavage look broken señor tired show fucking hate LA up to Seattle New York wicked yeah. I've always wanted to do it. Completely different. Can play PS4 whenever whatever want can't get fucking near Xbox One. Doom Matrix ass-fucked those guys with spider cock. Fuck spoke Dave never happen again you remember señor? Stink that good stuff interview very aggressive alright man yeah fucked tired have to fucking go you going yeah. You'll never see it. It's underneath the carpark. Spider cock.

Deg up.

Umbrella settled purple death on the monkeys in the white concrete shell, coming to America wall of deg stink good stuff. The beams opened to the southern United States a yellow deg ceiling. The monkeys ate each other tore grey skin from each other's backs melted to apish glue before the taco stand.

You look broken, señor.

I fucking hate LA. The sat nav crashed cried in deg car cast magic freeway filming for six weeks. I'll see how it goes.

Power is a rare thing. A rare resource.

Quin Benko returned from his meeting, his heart in his hand and blood on his chicken breast lips. He smelt all spicy nice his pockets full of spiders clutched two pieces of paper one in each fox hand.

He wants you to come, said Quin. He will take you to Brazil.

A black afro hardbody in peach striped bikini bottoms hulahooped in a heat haze. Window MILF didn't come when she fucked and the nice blonde waitress, white lace on CA tan, showed her how. Tiny tits squeaked white as blonde licked her cunt. Miami Vice, nice cut cock, leaned in the doorway till she sucked his bell while blonde lady, nice lady, licked her cunt toilet spoke Chinese in my ear not Kindle, not passport, just shoes all laptop all belt Chinese in the stall head over stall cock wrapped in tissue, my head over the top of the stall in the space where the Chinese woman speaker blue came split paper grunted like pig. Grey Miami Vice American blonde woman earrings pearl lace tits teen. Billy rolled his eyes and shat in the teen's mouth. Record traffic, and so great to see you. I love the concept. Best E3 ever. Great E3. Will definitely come again next year. Dairy free ice cream meatball sub Culver City. We call them bobbleheads. Same doctor shaves down below the doctor shaves them stick-thin then pumps up chest with pump cock. Pump it up. Made top-heavy bobbleheads shit in mouth. Teen hug pink pig spread legs iPhone. Charge your mobile devices thank you for recognising it's not the time I'm not going to say anything. Thank you, sir. Buck teeth teen cunt Hollywood. Billy shat mouth teen cunt. Old white French women black hair shoe white. Teen sucked spider cock mature ass fucked French grandma ass. Regime plus tards relax.

I'm glad we've reached a point of clarity, said Billy.

Pearls bounced from waves as Ira swam iridescence in all directions and the shore gone. Waves marbles pearls glowed in the lightning rain hissed soaked in the wells at the bottom of the blistered red doors. Lulu smoothed her skirt.

What I hate most about flies, she said, is when you see them humping.

She accented the final word, blood tumbling from cherry lips down over her chin. She dragged bone-white fingers across her shaved pubis, the snowless piste glowing green in the distance. Maggots tunnelled through the cubes of rotten meat in Link's bowl heap food atop jelly maggots.

I'll never tell anyone about this, she said. She cupped a handful of blood and submerged Ira's balls sucked the tip of his cock bit it till it bled semen blended with blood ran from her mouth down the shaft into the blood puddle balls maggots piste jumped Chalet Fleuri plaquettes de frein.

J'ai fait un rendez-vous avec la dentiste pour le vingt-et-un août, je crois. Il faut que j'aie à l'Allemagne pour travailler, malheureusement. Faut le changer. Je suis désolé.

The blue mask twitched as Loon strapped it on. Bloody baby arms radiated from her black ponytail, a small hand wiggling around her ear. Pools of tar smouldered behind cherry blossom glasses she tied the mask tight so her lipstick seeped through the green fabric and drizzled her neck what seems to be the problem.

Faut parlez lentement.

Evidemment. Pas de souci.

Loon rammed a steel spike into the centre of Ira's wisdom tooth and he bit into her fingers but she wouldn't let go he slid his hand up her jaguar tooth skirt and into the back of her knickers fingered her arsehole. She scraped against the enamel from the inside back down onto the nerve no no not the hooked spike emerged from where her hand used to be twenties posters of little black boys sucking sugar lumps the hand holding the drill sliced open pants pushed down into urethra repeatedly mashed the wisdom tooth nerve Ira worked three fingers into her rectum bent over his body to allow easier access. Metal inside his cock and mouth finger-fucked her anus chewed his hand disappeared into colon blood jetted from his lower lip. She gnawed his hand with her arse. He severed her fingers relieved the pain in his wisdom tooth she sheared the head from his penis pulled her knickers down and mouthed his headless erection fountains red paint little black boy sugar cube.

You lie about everything, you fucking greasy little shit.

Bat lamp street lamp wicker footstool edged in green taffeta. Blaue blumes bodyless crust a child's wicker chair quarter past fourteen in the mirror blue bottle red bells from the wrought iron china plate of marbles circular frog on a mahogany spiral cried tears of green. Red spotted dresser. Loon toyed with the hairs on Ira's chest smoothed the amethyst tears on his cheeks with her lips. Pea bowl for coffee and croissant jam violet lanterns peacock butterflies Sengalese soldier took his drink. Ring binder. Fire extinguisher. Bird feather sunrays collapsed like demolished buildings across the moon sheets. The golden frog grinned blank eyes and the dragon circled Ira's flask constricted its ejaculation. Ashtrays metal cake cased blue ashtrays bronze candlesticks in happy families and cobwebs above the canals. Loon pushed him from the soaking bed with a smile and packed him off to Cologne.

Grunting, grimacing, James the Knife scraped his feet down the side of the convention centre Radisson interview heart decorated his satchel in pig blood straight from the liver. A German family trembled in the main hangar don't camp here smashed waves against Blizzard's stand Diablo Paris I knew I had to make the effort they even cunt WiFi I scream cunt I can't get inside.

Call the Frenchman, Curly yelped, leaping over the turnstiles to punch through the crowd. Tory made the trip from Leipzig her torso split open from her neck to cunt blonde hair piled around elf eyes. Blizzard one-to-one maybe we should steer away from that. James ate a bowl of sugar by sticking his face straight down against the table dubbed Simpsons it's actually pretty good. Take us home, Ira. What was the take-home from the Sony conference chips mayonnaise Jenny blowjob Michael invited Ira back to his apartment on the west side of Cologne fucked his mouth muscled him to the carpeted ground and rubbed shit on his chest chips mayonnaise. Two slim Arab boys squeezed soft ice cream between luscious lips outside the launderette this is Milanese beef. Good, yes? Salty beef. Ira took one of the Arabs into his mouth his golden cock right up to the balls which were small and emitted a faint odour of running sweat and cheap soap. The other Arab greased Ira's asshole with an old tube of KY and slid inside large cock thick at the base. Ira moaned as the two Arabs grabbed an end each and exercised his holes with as much force as their slender frames could manage the streets of Rome prego you certainly know you're in Germany. The angular airport lights cold flags flew over the gate. You haven't got a fucking clue, Ira. The burning shame of impotence. Sexyland. Gaunt muscles stared at freezing clouds honey milk do I remember you? Blood oozed down the stairs Fernsehturm. You can't use that in here, Ira.

Cadarves needs me, he said, turning the spoon between his teeth.

Lulu snorted. Cadarves is everything without you. You haven't got a fucking clue.

I have to get on that plane.

That gate is closed, sir.

Cabbage and oranges piled behind mouldy windows grandmother swollen feet pushed through the vodka bottle security guards bullied electronics shop doors. You can't fucking go in there, man. No English megalithic blocks of despair mounded against yellow hate vodka and beer on the streets ran with diarrhoea last month the heating went off and these flats didn't have any hot water for weeks. Soviet yellow bath Ira's Cadbury's Flake moment span skirts in the bulletproof bar you're not in the Zone.

She's very good, sir. Stay in your room all night before you go to the reactor tomorrow.

White face didn't permit the taking of photos. A head extended from her belly nipped Ira as she fucked him yellow water flake whirling skirts catfish the size of a man. No competition there. Everything dead red forest don't walk over there dolls in the text books this is the swimming pool murals of hope.

I bet the fucking guides put this shit here just for something to see.

I want to fuck a wolf. A radioactive wolf. In a disused helicopter.

Jerry cans of beans ate slowly while the Vikings drank vodka shouted and vomited on the bus. If you develop cancer in the future this has nothing sarcophagus fuck a wolf white, tight-faced woman black bowlhead giant catfish they have to leave the site if the radiation badge too much exposure leaned over the bridge fed the giant catfish reactor tomb background it's amazing.

It isn't amazing. You are now in the Zone. You can't go there. They'll fucking kill you.

Some fucking prick. Ira bought the two-headed hooker for the second night brought one of the drunk Vikings back to his room so he could fuck the second head while he took care of white lady asshole yellow water Cadbury's Flake. Ira with the hard sell. Jennifer flicked a prostitute from the end of her mule.

Thank you, boys. Go on. Put your dick in his fucking mouth. Don't be gay. I can see China down there.

Ira stroked Cadarves on the arm metal stream of vomit fuelled Carnaby Street tweed melted left up right down, He pulled away and Ira began to cry. Cadarves rolled his eyes and handed over a bright blue tissue made from the skin of a thousand virgin boys. Dancing boys. You do realise this is a gay club? Yes, rocketman, you should get ready now. You're the publisher: what plans do you have for the site?

To be perfectly frank, James, I don't have the first fucking clue.

Hacked to death. I've already had her, and the simple truth, Jennifer, is that I can't do this anymore. The only person in the entire company without a desktop. The molten shame of working on the hot desk practically in the corridor what the fuck is rubber lips doing there it wasn't just the odd line.

Say, for instance, that you and I were to like each other. I don't think it would work. You're going to wake up in a fucking ditch.

She laughed, but Ira doubted she found anything particularly funny took a table knife and began to cut at his own wrist windows opened surrounded him focused on his torn skin flash text scorched the air: misogynist. She ground his face into the boiling gravy get me fucking out of here give me a job should I give you a fucking chance? Product-by-product basis. Well done. I doubt we'll book, to be honest.

I had no idea what I was doing was wrong.

Berlin's bulletholes hardened in the background.

I don't believe you, Ira.

Analytics is fine for me graph goes up. I'd like to thank Ira for being really, really fucking scary. Loon glared at him over cellulose frames.

That doesn't mean you can wait.

Blue pills cocaine Lulu this isn't going to work. Ira wept in a shopping centre lines off her tits pools of lust quick powder red bar full of maggots spilled over the crates. I'll buy you a drink. The barman rested a bear paw on Ira's shoulder.

I'm really sorry, said Ira.

It's fine, son, said the Irishman. I'm more worried about you.

Lulu stormed into the kitchen get up. Cat up a tree.

I think we're done here, said Ira.

FOUR ———

The Swiss border guard brown skin mace in cock place, gun with not a scratch. Aged about twenty-five, at a guess, with smooth hair and sucker lips. Ira wanted to kiss him.

Guten tag, he said no flicker of humour. Ira fumbled his card into the slot and refused to look at him again. The douane dumped the green motorway sticker into his metal tray and returned stare to the side of his Perspex booth. Ira said thank you in German and barged out, alarming a Spanish trucker. Mountain green trees and jets of water combed the wheat. Genève but Ira missed and barrelled through tunnels as Corrine summoned Ira immediately on his reaching Annecy met all the traffickers homeless couples slept on cardboard with Nike children takeaway pizza spicy. Annecy real warm parted the shutters. Two sucked intertwined oysters from a black wire table on a balcony over a lazy canal.

Mieux comme ça?

Ben oui.

Corrine guarded the red room and all visited for deg. White hair, black eye; all deg par elle. She lived on the première étage in a bis on Rue Royale stamped ticket for cheap parking. The deuxième étage held deg and seeds in paper wax bags. Corrine's dope always was the best in the south, harder than Toulouse Anna's. Hoarded the deg and the green room Pyrénées smaller Alps followed Mont Blanc tunnel Genève then Chamonix. She readied the big deg drop.

Parfait, Ira, she said.

Cream hair skirt flapped round ankle bracelet palm tree red headdress wrapped in gold, her brown skin smooth as rectal wall two fingers pain on her face. Cock in her ass then out and shit on her lips. Came on her teeth lapped at the bones like ice cream. Fucked ass again. Ass welled around cock head like chewing orange: came in ass and she liked it.

Parfait, Ira.

Ira perched in the red room to discuss the deg. She held a mighty load.

It'll fill the car and right stink, so no going back to see the brown friend with the ass mace.

She flicked on a small window and tapped for maths. Ira jail life if ass mace man got a go, but big enough to end the Paris game. Tuft hair on a clean cunt. Ira closed the curtains over the river and jerked his cock up. She told Ira that if he wanted a man to use a condom as she didn't want to catch any horrible diseases her words. Another man in the bed would scare her, she said. Lulu asked if Ira'd like another woman to join and he said no. Cock right up and bright blonde rimmed Asian while she fingered shaved pussy. Pulled down hard on scrotum until it turned blue. Corrine rimmed Ira while jerking blue cock punched balls hard made Ira cry then come. Window said take the deg, ripe nice and lovely buds, very strong four sacks of Bubble Gum for Ira gunfire kaleidoscope flowers brown octagram blue. A sadhu's hand signed behind his back the Alps here down the alley. Gap tooth pills for a fiver took two. She seemed younger than he no older than twenty. He was more muscular black against her white. Did both the pills down the alley off Oxford Street amazed at how fast the crowds dissipated. Midnight slumped against anti-climb the speed promised to support the tablets. Ira had already taken a bunch to drink otherwise felt confident he could make a double peak thumped to the ground blue night orange highlights black cobbles no stars London, London, always the same ground wet no one cared. The girl smiled at Ira, that big-mouthed wide upper smile nowhere near any deg movement no deg on pills or charlie flattened out any deg tube and blackened the back to form a mirror shaped to straighten the upper user's image. Backs against red brick black cobbles orange mousse above the roofs. Want some of this? The black man used his lighter to melt a milky crystal onto a screen of cigarette ash in a glass pipe. After it liquefied he sucked it bright white then passed the pipe to the girl. They began to glow cornsilk. He offered the pipe to Ira away from the crowds dead through the tunnel on Oxford Street beyond the bricks the man wouldn't let him hold it so he put the end in his mouth and sucked as the lighter cooked the solid ash mixture to an orange star creamy plastic smoke filled the pipe and Ira's lungs and neck became red then white. Off the pipe black man watched him with a jelly grin as he finished and Ira and the girl and the man sat in soaked silence. Cobbles blue not black and the mousse bubbled crimson. The Spoonfaces turned away and sobbed. Ira shunned with the spiders and maggots on the blue Oxford Street flags. Bond in the mirror night bus. The girl, acne skin and bobbed bleached hair, sat behind Ira in the top seat her skeletal forearms locked over folded knees whispering to the man in the yellow smoky light of the upper deck. Ira turned round occasionally and they smiled back. The girl definitely wanted to fuck him. She giggled the double tablet pushed Ira away on a plane far from the Spoonfaces and the Cats, away from the rubs and the no photos please to the black orange void nothing but streamers. Eyes opened two mirrors where there was one chameleon top deck of the bus door in Highbury cashpoint. Don't worry, said the man. They knocked on the door peace and love. Old black man entrance other black people inside. Dreads down to his ass, so thin he appeared to be starving, wearing pair of jeans with no shoes no top. No lampshades no furniture everyone sat on the littered floor smoking rocks. Peace and love, Gary, peace and love. Who the fuck is this? I known 'im time. Money how long you known this guy met him tonight I fucking knew it smoke this give me money I don't have any more money give me the fucking money. He rifled through Ira's pockets and the white girl disappeared. Ira had no intention of stopping him ripped out his passport. Look over there, man. He's fucking mugging him. Dread told him to stop but now checked the papers please.

Is he a fucking pig?

The man threw the passport into Ira's lap through the mirror twenty minutes previously nailed self to chair not there Ira unable to cry smoke this cashpoint money taken out a hundred quid already girl couldn't stop shaking. No more than eighteen. Thick brown lips and bulging eyeballs head shook from side to side like fitting couldn't speak she couldn't speak eyes on verge of popping, teeth clacked together squeaky lizard noises hair rose vertically from her brow which the crack pushed up into a terrible facelift. Ira rubbed her back and said everything's going to be alright and she shook less but remained mute. Ira kept saying over and over again it's going to be alright and other smokers watched on no one intervened mollified. Architecture student smoked crystals shared with Ira laughed alone found it hard to believe the young man could do his work when he journeyed every evening to the no furniture house.

I can handle it, said the boy.

The cashpoint only allowed Ira take out another twenty red brick plastic doors surrounded the courtyard rock on. Break the spell, baby, break the spell. Smoked crack off gauze embedded in the bottom of a brandy miniature. Break the spell, baby, and rock on. Bleached girl still smiled at fat white Ira. Break the spell. Baby sun false dawn off license St Paul's road pulled black cans from the fridge. Ira took a twenty note from his pocket and the man snatched it from his hand. The shopkeeper threatened to call the police.

That's my money, said Ira.

You owe me that, said the man. Come on, he said to the giggling girl, and they vanished from the shop the shopkeeper saying dear me and looked on Ira with such pity, fat white Ira, that molten crack tears draped his lower eyelids some pound coins left in the bottom of his pocket so he bought two black cans and sat on a park bench near Highbury & Islington tube station a seat to himself and some cigarettes perfectly happy. Sacks of crack.

What the fuck are you talking about? said the man.

Just imagine how many rocks Gary has.

Shut up.

Perfectly happy sat there in the warming London sun with his Kestrel Super chain-smoking Marlboro Red. No deg or mirror just the yellow light and the trees red bus rumbled wiped spunk on a watercolour and rubbed with filthy fingers so lumps of jelly formed into patches of cloud and saline drew up the trunks to screeching blue. Ira needed to make a decision about going to work. He could either go or not, but seeing as he'd missed many days previously he fixed on going. Half a gram of speed hidden in his sock and finished his beer before riding the train into the centre of town. Commuters in polished leather shoes read bad books and applied eye-liner tallow light shallow breath mirror highlighted Ira's rolls stinking fat dirty Ira in the office. The first in. Tungsten strip-lights turned his Mac desk island.

You alright, Ira?

I've been smoking crack all night.

You don't do things by halves.

A nice cold beer. Deg window nowhere and never a mirror with beer, a nice cold beer. Soho bar muscled men drank coloured liquids and touched each other blue lights poppers until they could barely speak. Ira and Graham spent expense account money on leather sofa credit card. Just put in the receipts. So much poppers. Three for two we're closing now. Eric B & Rakim in Chinatown let me have a look. Fuck you, man. It's cool. Let him look. That work for you, blud? Ira fumbled with the plastic wrapper. Nice rocks inside. Yeah, it's cool. He handed over notes. You want a pipe? Nah. Ira had no idea where this man came from and Graham baffled a doorway. Eric B & Rakim on the main street in Chinatown but he commanded the pipe. Smoked another rock. Get your man out of there. That's just a fucking tip, man. I ain't no joke.

White or brown?

Both.

Good man.

Wire hair mushroom hands false dawn got to get me some fucking money. The pipe commander melted crack into the ash and sprinkled a pinch of heroin onto the top of the mixture and he wouldn't touch it because of the brown. Ira smoked the lot food war. How much do you do a day? Don't fucking ask him that, man. Lifted up his t-shirt as though it had been soaked in mud to reveal Ira a syringe and needle tucked into his belt the green first hint of dawn pressed the gazebo and the orange streetlights purple slush brown blood. Ira's heart and eyes fluttered bore pipe commander. Kept his works on display against scarred gut, which bore no fat as though starving. Some shelter. Pasty ghouls drank methadone in a flat-pack kitchen. You do methadone? No, I don't do it. I hardly ever do smack. Maybe you can hook me up with a graphics job. Smoke this. Graham laughed. The methadone ghost didn't laugh. Graham stopped laughing. Ira grabbed Graham's hand and they made excuses the night outside as black as only London nights can be. The towering horror of Bermondsey a blue leather sofa Sonic the Hedgehog vodka. The station blue sofa nothing else in the house apart from a huge television check out my melody. Evil black the Bermondsey stacks where the killers are. Ira put a call into the Spoonfaces. Radar antenna on a bee wouldn't answer the deg windows filed away between velvet dividers to prevent breakages. The Spoonfaces dragged their feet to the intergalactic velvet tower dirge while the channel pulsed with Ira's call under the demon breath of Bermondsey. Danced with the speaker. Ira called and called, puts his head back and groaned, vomited on Tube. Graham sniffed up and moved on.

Spoonfaces long, long gone to Newcastle just an hour up the coast. They brought a motorbike into the house and stole all his kitchenware while the feathers pinkened.

Drugs are fucking expensive here, said Ira. Speed's seven quid a teenth in Wrexham.

Oz fuck, said the angel.

Lines of chalky whiz levitated from the back of a CD case and a trip corner blew deg drank brandy from the bottle. Ira couldn't open the tubes. The Spoonfaces monitored the situation from Outback heights with shaking heads and slow tuts. Condemned apartment block shower sprayed scalding water in your face two bottles cider super-strength on the way home forty cents for noodles write write write. I'm going to write my way out of this. Drank cider wrote violent British fantasies and posted them to Feather.

Fruit worked her way around hand cramps and cider gone ate noodles. Slogged miles to the Serbians no money for anything other than wine boxes. Ira hadn't eaten for three days, but thinner at least not fat anymore for the homeless Thatcher murder slept wet under freezing mattress while outside the prostitutes thought we were just going to have a chat. You take a spa with one of our girls. Don't you have a card? High heels tapped neon stripes in Sydney puddles. Do you like that? Ira's cock disappeared up the backside of a fat drunkard. Didn't listen to Sheryl Crowe much. What are you doing this afternoon? Don't worry: I've been sterilised. Parakeets rainbow of sand and lemon delivered leaflets.

She's deaf, said the Serbian, a bald skittle picking his teeth with his Australian citizenship. Ira wasn't sure. It'll cost two thousand dollars. What's the fucking matter, man? She's deaf. She won't be able to hear you and she'll never moan.

I don't have any money, said Ira.

You can pay it off with deliveries. Don't you want to stay?

Half bottles of white wine in the fridges hairy porn in plastic bags. Indian light cut himself deep in the sink on a brutal Saturday and the big Serbian pulled him into the muddy back-room sloshed

Johnny Walker over Andrej's slashed palm. Andrej was a sniper in Serbia. He ate nothing but potatoes for two years. He'll laugh at anything, watch: Hey, Ira: fuck you. Ira laughed. He took the Serbian's car out past the barriers but had no money to pay, so smashed through deg upside the head Blue Mountains. No money to do anything but look.

Ira opened only two deg tubes during his time in Racistland, and continued with his ecstasy and alcohol mission to disastrous effect. Never stopped drinking. One pair of jeans and a Welsh flag across the mantelpiece in the furnitureless pub next to the Serbians' restaurant we won't be taking Paris from here. The Spoonfaces sent a pigeon. Ira woke one morning to find it shitting on a shelf in the corner of his yellow room, flaking paint thirty dollars a week. A starving boy on the Opera House steps, goggling dizzy at the infinite blue. The pigeon surveyed Ira, perched on his shoulder home for a bong, but the pills prevented the opening of the deg tube twenty dollars each got them from some English cunt married to her sister.

The Spoonfaces channelled rumbling invisible bird while Ira phoned home to the mother about how he should become a millionaire, stinking in his pair of jeans in a phone box using all his credit every day to call anyone, writing endless letters wanted to come home. The Serbian pushed him to the floor to see an apple and a tray he was supposed to clean up but hadn't, pushed him down into the floor pressed his face on the tiles. The swimmer tittered. Spoonface pigeon cried up in the rafters dear me. Fruit's sister pissed in the corner of his hotel room and cried when she left.

I can't, she said. I understand, but Fruit would kill me.

Ira wiped the tears from her vaulted cheeks. Are you sure you want to come in my car with me? The pigeon followed Ira's bus to Outback Queensland, fought Koreans at the pool hall. Stay in the fucking car. The pigeon glowed green and Ira sat back down. Kangas play dusty in the morning. I'm not your fucking mother.

Ira, at this point, was as far away from Cadarves as it's possible to be with a mercenary on a fucking fruit farm picked oranges by the ton. I haven't eaten for three days and may steal a can of Coke, you know, for the sugar. Fishing rod at the side of the road yard sale sunglasses to pawn shops for five dollars increased over cost time. Ten dollars a day enough to buy wine and a bag of chips. You'll regret that in a few years. No nutrients, said the doctor. He has a cock like a fucking tree trunk and we both come three times a night. I'm a fucking man. I like guys' stuff. I like sport and PlayStation. I'm not a bigot, you know? You stay away from those trees.

I was working as a mercenary, said the mercenary. We'll steal his pills in the next hospital. We repurposed tractor parts.

Sack cloth pouched, snakes in the trees slithered into the bathroom with me to fuck but she didn't toothy redhead some eighteen-year-old Irish girl. Bent her over in front of a mirror while others watched wanked and fucked her pussy. She panted as the others squirted jism over her legs. Ira wiped the tip of his cock on her shitty asshole then pushes inside while she licked her own face in the mirror. The pigeon nodded back to the Spoonfaces. I left a cap I stole in a barmaid's hole and I never went there again. Licked her cunt on the toilet after she'd finished pissing. I thought you were going to take her home but it seemed as though she'd had enough.

Facking 'ell, eh. We got some foreigners 'ere.

Reg the kanga-killer tapped the head of his cock through a pair of khaki hotpants wraparound sunglasses raw corn poured into the top of his cowboy boots.

You fucking bastard. Rejection's watery eyes.

You appear to have given my phone number to every slut in Sydney. Sally knocked a joint together.

I'm going to have a tattoo done on my back next week. D'you wanna come?

Red worked the days in a one-door dry cleaner. She hugged Ira when he visited performed as a hooker in west Sydney at night. Passion on ice. Don't do that. I get paid a lot of fucking money. Ira made his meeting with the landlord on time. He's nice clapped Arthur. After the dirt and starvation on the stinking racist Sydney streets wait till you see the whites of their eyes. They're not like the fucking blacks in Europe, eh. They just cause trouble. They strip the pipes from the fucking houses, eh.

Ira opened a tube in Melbourne direct to Spoonfaces around the pigeon with acid they bought from some posh waiter at the gentlemen's club. He scrubbed the dishes and sang about heroin in the empty kitchen. Tom shouted at his girlfriend litter blew and gaped that's as far as you go. Not safe outside. He fucked with Fruit in Sydney but don't tell her, for fuck's sake. She doesn't know anything about it.

The Lord of the Spoonfaces called time. Daga Spoonface centrum a cluster of wires and levels and the underground Spoonface network built into secret ski lift spoon-level encased in lead to keep it away from the Cats. Pigeon shitty asshole. Tom and Ira splashed naked in the tub with Gwendolyn. Ira stood up in front of her soapy cock but she didn't bite sucked Tom's tongue in front of her calm down.

Read out the pigeon report, commanded the Lord of the Spoonfaces. Doctor Loon glared and wiped the bird's heart and liver over the head of his knocking penis.

We can grow the meat, hissed Loon. The flavour needs work, but I'm confident in the consistency. Ira's progress, however, is a different matter. The Thatcher construction was embarrassing at best, and the Cats know it. Give me another pigeon to fuck.

Paddington died at midnight and Ira crept around the streets snorting deg from cash machines. Prostitutes searched for business under the Manchester arches. Black woman angular factories eyeglass windows degree in Lapland: the sea was terrifying.

Looking for business, love? Ira's cock stayed limp. Have a fiddle around in here, she said, and pushed his hand into her knickers. Her lips dry but Ira felt the inside of her pink on the inside they're all pink on the inside those are mine smoked Navy cigarettes in the BMW. Ira had never had sex with a black woman before.

Here, she said. A warehouse garage drunk students retched past on the shortcut between bars. She touched her toes in front of him and he pushed into her but couldn't maintain any kind of firmness tears. She stood and pulled the condom from the end of his cock with a weak snap. The night filth around him pasty white legs streaked pants puddle on the floor next to stinking socks. She stiffened his cock with both hands and began to wank him worked very drunk. She cups his balls filthy darkness out on the street students yelled and looked into the garage could see her jerking his white cock. I'm coming. That's good, she said. Ejaculated over her fingers. Once he'd finished she threw tissues at him gone and the white papers fluttered down in the darkness like snowflakes as sparkling party-goers crowded on the warehouse street. Anal Street.

You didn't think I'd let you go?

His cheeks sandpapered Ira's but his cock remained too soft to penetrate. Ira sprayed his face back on the bus. You're not in fucking Wales now, Ira. Boy, could she suck. You licked my balls with great tenderness. A bar of lard from the fridge coated the head of his cock and the shaft in animal fat penetrated Curlew's ass. He screamed real good an ass virgin. Malcolm pulled down on his blue balls while Ira slid his dick right up to the base and Curlew slapped his hands on the table. Ira came hard in Curlew's ass, pulled out so Malcolm could suck the shit and jism and lard from his crinkling purple cock head. Does anyone want a cup of tea? There's such a thing as common decency, said Loon.

Ira: get on the bed.

Loon white hair waistcoat withdrew his cock grey white truncheon and the yellow light of the pigeon chamber cast him sick that's quite a smile. Ira's cock came up large. Loon's thighs flabby white sick yellow. He formed a fist around the shaft of Ira's cock and slapped him hard on the balls then hoiked his knees up and spat on his asshole slid his dick all the way inside. Ira cried sick yellow white.

That's it, Ira, said Loon. It'll all be over soon.

Loon fucked him hard in the ass for many days as Ira searched for the deg wall. Once sick of the Spoonfaces, he now scoured the dustless void. He maintained constant dialogue with the pigeon while Loon fucked his face such a pretty smile. The pigeon took out a mortgage with the Spoonfaces Cats large chains on which the rank file Spoonfaces fiddled with their velvet robes and stroked the Cats the market quarter where the Cats sold their deg tubes. A city of metal boxes and mud streets garage in Manchester brothel Ira could never find again fucked some man in a corniced bedroom in front of a bus stop somewhere in Salford. He held him close, rubbed his stubble on his cheeks and refused to let him go. Ira strained against his muscles but he was strong enough to keep Ira in his spider. Loon slapped him across the ass with the head of his cock, sprayed semen into his eyes and across his twitching asshole. He severed his cock with an axe and split the turtle open with a machete, then wiped his crusting semen on the North London flat's padded red curtains.

It'll all be over soon, Ira.

Unconscious in a doorway don't ask him how much he does behind a clutch of black bags in a Soho alleyway. Impossible to get a cab with no money, no crack, black bags rats leakage fluid. He reversed the charges to Lulu via the mother.

We're going to close this down, said Loon.

Rémy screamed down the phone at Chas over his inability to speak French. You live in France so you should make an effort, he said, but Chas couldn't understand the words the meaning all that really matters. I learned well, he told Ira, and now I'm a qualified ramoneur. Ira nodded and turned the black Limousin loam, prepping deg beds for the greenhouse. Chas fixed the poêle à bois, sorted the through-draft turned the water off. We'd just had a few bottles of wine and got rid of some guests. We assumed it was an emergency, someone calling so late in the evening. There was a leak in the cave, said Ira. I didn't know what to do.

Chas applied flame-retardant paint to the fire-proof board he secured around the flue and advised Ira to put a piece of metal sheeting on the floor in case any embers escaped. Chas is dead now. Cancer killed him. This saddened the Cats. Make an effort.

Fox femur lichen-ball.

Deer skull broken heart.

Je t'aime.

The storm flooded down as Ira and Lulu waited for Jim and the wheel-bases. Deg dug up house packed and Cadarves already headed out east. All windows and doors wide he's angry, said Ira, but he should have said she. She's angry. The Cats and Spoonfaces mingled on the cubes, visibility down to metres. Garden drowned rain metal pearl drops metres in air houses vanished Cats slashed at Ira on the tiles pushed back lightning. Jim isn't going anywhere. The grey quilt. Corrèze, a green velvet cushion the Spoonfaces stitched down to run rivers. Pipes burst all the world's water fell on Ira and Lulu: she's angry left deg east. Colin the builder, denim dungarees and paint-flecked glasses, guarded the iron gate as the storm masked the sloped castle on the other side of the street. Molten grey nose grey hair. He smoked a cigar and rain hissed on its tip. His lenses water eyes steam rose burned like the Devil he is Devil he is Satan. He grinned at Ira and Lulu water and blood on his teeth and smoke cigar tore lightning thunder cannon river on teeth asphalt smoked.

Good luck, he said, and evaporated steam.

Cadarves and the Spoonfaces made a visit to Deg4 and Deg3 sat in the deg circles sucked on the helo-pipes fused at forehead by spoons deg cigar pipe replaced mouth through eye poked eyeball out took deg smoke direct to brain. Even Cadarves was so far along the deg tube it became impossible to point it in any meaningful direction, but the Spoonfaces confirmed achievement of the correct level to gain entry to the third stage and mount the Paris challenge. Crop up good. The Spoonfaces returned to the Cats and Cadarves's eyes still didn't work. After a day spent peering through the three windows, Ira collapsed in the living room phone pane. He dragged Twitter vertically with right thumb, reading and rereading messages, pulling the page up and down and refreshed then up and down again. Ira retweeted things he'd read three or four times, then through the window at the script of the app itself to see past the illusion pixels constructed image page on a screen no longer a screen but a tactile malleable device not a piece of glass. Ira closed the app, flicked Android to the left and immediately reopened to see the same icons from a few seconds earlier. He grunted hypnotised dog wanted to get stoned. Lulu shuffled around him throwing sad eyes, hanging washing in front of the fire on clothes airers flicked the screen up and down with his thumb, and notions of writing or reading or playing a game or going outside to stand in the cold and look at the stars were eaten by the window, the flicking, and his wife's sad eyes as she went about the business of keeping their house in order.

Plenty places more remote than that. We're on the edge of the wilderness here. There isn't a light for ten clicks, Cadarves. Buckle up. We're rolling to Turbo Town.

FIVE ·········——··

A bottleful of grasshoppers made more sense than Cadarves's arm lost green steepness prevented the deer descending. No signal for the screen. My father taught me how to survive in the woods skin rabbit ferret pursenet. Break a leg down here, Cadarves, and no one's coming to get you. Darling, don't let your bag roll down how to use a compass. Here's the firebreak we're going northwest line up the map like this dropped right off pain in the knees verticality first Mars bar. You said no animals come down here but the bean can was snuffled up in the morning. Sleep with a combat knife real tight, sweetheart. Moths bats next I'll teach you how to use a gun the coming insurrection. Shotgun stopping power six years old I told her not to hesitate: do not hesitate: pull the trigger: shoot to kill. Ecosystem anarchy is the only form of social management capable of producing a realistic future for life on Earth and to that end potatoes chillis manure beau jardin mec de la campagne. First we attack the trains, my love, incendiary devices on the carriages in Gare de Nord mix sticky powder burned straight through the metal onto the seats below fireball plastic bottles filled with napalm petrol dissolved polystyrene can't get that shit off at all.

Carrots beans filled the grid used a supporting fence of twine maggots gold beetle.

The insects needed to be reported to the authorities in the UK. Bottle bucket of soapy water infestation pulled them off drowned in the suds. Give them a chance they'll take your entire potato harvest. Lulu worked her hands to blood to ensure the plants cropped. These are aggressive chickens Limousin hens peck your fucking face off. Can't go anywhere near them. The cock pulled all the feathers from the backs of the hens hard work. Took the better part of a year bloody idiots. He didn't stop till he hit the sea. Bottles of syruped apricots.

Cheeto stalled his camping car against a quartz wall high in the Pyrénées. Blake's 7 remake octopus followed good conceit conflate spanned out through the windows spread among friends of the thesaurus trope. Down in the valley and up on the crystal highs the Spoonfaces watched over the peaks and troughs kept the window signal minimised. Cats sailed the spaces between the stars poodled away in golden coils hair lay in a circle, a ring of popularity. The harpy's elongated piggish body writhed beneath its transparent maggot surface and with each growth sprouted a new set of breasts thick black glasses stained speckled purple jeans maggots sucked up the semen and ass everybody fucks everybody dies suckled at the nipple as she wailed in electric aphorisms. Flabby teenagers climbed from breast layer to breast layer closer and closer to the snapping crème de menthe teeth. Beneath the breasts, in the blackness underneath the swelling sodomy circle, festered the Field of Cunts, the lowest caste, that of the traitors; it swarmed with icy members tongue-fucked while the pig maggot squirted up their noses as she cackled hair frothed and curled from the higher rings slapped at her breasts and the more popular members of the circle complete with their own lesser rings suckled rotten milk from the teats lapped at clits like Labradors fat dogs ate shit played games free hugs incendiary devices on carriage roofs spread through the void whirls of spilt jism galaxy Cats circled mirror infinity hyper-giant cunt-lickers sucked brown dwarfs to create windows tit-strings dropped out vacuum the circles clumped into galactic formations on their cunt stalks cock mountains each phallus speared the anus of some simpering student glasses pout. A grande pair of moustaches and a cross-eyed waiter with a stoop composez votre snow-cone desperados a black-haired, slop-jugged biker smoked an electronic cigarette. Megacity monochrome print sunglasses shaped down silver across the centre vesuvio plein les yeux. Chairs arranged wooden tombstone thirty-degree red-faced slug maggot barstool Alsace sauerkraut cream bra crucifix knitted crimson sweater across his hunchback paced between the Twitter stars Cat afterbirth remplir the most sour black and the Spoonfaces in their white robes and hidden feet faces concave under blackball eyes. Red-face rolled his trolley merci hunchback furious at the heat rings rotated and hummed as the tit-suckers lapped in unison. Hang on the retweets each wave of presses shot a meteor across the rings fly wouldn't leave her arm. Too hot for the hunchback. Fern white shirt splayed to show the golden crucifix free WiFi spider-haired electronic smoker with a bald podgy man in an angel shirt smoked real tobacco. She avoided it with all the success of a Cat ignoring a mouse. An African staggered under the weight of fifty hats brown wallet rainbow. Hunchback refused to revisit Ira's table. Tits everywhere cock up grande moustache and hunchback sweated at the back of the bar grey teeth petit café oui bien sûr verre d'eau have to stay away for three nights instead of two.

Cadarves needs the deg seeds final operation Turbo Town needs the deg split the windows needs the seeds, Lulu said.

Lulu and Ira unlocked the apartment's door off the canal into a tunnel through to the blue bedroom double bed fridge single heater for making soup. Clarisse, a European teenager Lulu seduced in one of the quieter deg cafés, said she preferred the less populated canals. Davy's gray unblemished skin dimpled slightly at the nose. Spoonface café verre d'eau oui bien sûr. Clarisse tossed glossy hair over white bra back Lulu stripped off lace and pushed Clarisse back onto the bed licked nipples blue bed wallpaper squirmed maggots. Twitter suns encircled a glass pipe Ira lit choked up deg strong enough to be illegal even there. Lulu slid down to Clarisse's shaved cunt stripped pants bald licked clit power deg and the two women didn't appear to care when Ira opened a high definition window white cap streamed YouTube grande moustaches white ass headed for the toilet the Instagram windows spread rapidly man charcoal suit.

Loon swung through Turbo Town's central arcade, a gothic boulevard of patisseries and tailors, and tapped chewing gum from the tip of his brogue with a sword cane. Thick red lipstick smoked Pall Mall. Ira grabbed the attendant by the arm: il est où rose impression. Loon's hair half brown stripped to bald patch at the rear, molten steel glasses black suit white shirt black tie emerged from the back of the bar. Grande moustache chewed a filterless cigarette bent over a stool spat on his hairy ass then fucked it. Hunchback leapt up onto the bar and cheered, crunched grey teeth in grande moustache's puckered face. Loon's suit proved inappropriate for the heat. Hunchback forgot about the temperature. Stupid hat grey slick green black fat print grande moustache dried white vest Clarisse squirted blood into Lulu's mouth. Windows crushed out Twitter over the canals light Ira's sun large twinkle pig woman simply outraged passed deg strips round beer shooting stars. Ira's sun expanded red giant swallowed piggy's piffling nebula unbelievable it's not obvious how dehumanising pornography is to young women.

Lulu took a breadknife and sliced open her belly with Clarisse's fists on the handle. They sawed through her abdominals as they licked each other's tongues deg choked the room Clarisse pushed Lulu's face back onto her clit as intestines, bursting with maggots, spilled out onto blonde hair. A smart couple. Perrier is naturally carbonated.

We'd better hurry up, said Ira, raising his eyebrows. Get her fucking guts back in, for fuck's sake. Pigs coming this is Dammer no one gives a fuck deg up, said Lulu, and demanded Ira fuck her ass while Clarisse compressed his scrotum. She opened ass Clarisse whole tugged down on Ira's blue balls blue bed blue room canals swans deg all the fucking way up to the sack her small rectum full of Ira's Buddha cock and a smile like a nuclear meltdown. Clarisse slapped her bald cunt slapped Lulu's tight ass first target is five lengths one after another in and out to the head. Clarisse slipped two fingers into Ira's ass Lulu screamed at Ira to fuck harder pounded her ass rimmed with maggots. Fuck me harder in ass ringed maggots Ira sprayed lumpy blood into Lulu's mouth blue room blue light Lulu drank up wiped lips. I absolutely detest when you see two flies humping, she said with the emphasis on the final word.

Now you can fuck her, said Lulu, taking up the window stream Dammer alight largest sun in Twitterverse Instagram on lock-down, melt-down, unable to suffer weight of window on les Pays Bas, sinking the country into the North Sea tulip fields drinking up the salt water dykes fractured bubbles of gas leaked out across the Channel. Lulu punched Ira's ass so he could better fuck Clarisse hands tied to the top of the blue bed. Maggots ate her dead eyes the Spoonfaces held an emergency session. Loon vanished stupid cap.

We shouldn't have killed her, said Ira.

Holland's dykes split. The North Sea and its fourteen remaining cod washed down into Rotterdam flattening a school and removing the watery town hall. Fedora blue vest nipples like ship rivets mirror sunglasses beautiful straight cock thick as a double shot glass and filled with green syrup for injection. Hairless back muscles rippled under Ira's fingers. You're too tight for the green shot, he said. Please fuck me please fuck me green shot too tight three grams of speed heavy balder with beers for eyes replaced the hunchback. A garçon with such beautiful skin. His friend held Ira's ass wider green shot insertion. Cock like a table leg in right up to his eyes. Fill green sirop kiwi bad for your teeth. Drowned in spunk. His nipples had no hair. A lover's smile. Lulu warned you to wear a condom.

Loon dropped the paper onto the café table and squinted at the headline: Amsterdam drowns after Twitter murder. Ira and Lulu transmitted Clarisse's deg tunnel to the forkeyes encore un café. If you wouldn't do it for me why do they do it to you? Loon fingered his bald patch hands buzzed with caffeine erected sign for the deg. Fucking dying here. Forkeyes sucked up Clarisse's tunnel supernova crushed out half the suns puce fire raged across the dome. Maggots shone bright white. A summer sky the colour of periwinkles pink vests pale blue vests mahogany awnings maggots roasting in the August sun. Loon scattered coins on the tabletop and spat on the cold tiled floor.

It's necessary to call just before you arrive to collect the code to unlock the key box to unlock the apartment backed onto the canal.

Starbucks breakfast. Clarisse rolled up some pure deg paid for by Ira as Lulu sank into the corner, her face full of green smoke I love you. Flexed his hands accepted les bieres des hauts nos vins des moments. Ira caressed Clarisse's hand. Lulu shadowed her corpse almost entirely consumed by maggots windows twitched through the blue air like flies hornets big wasps out into the sea submerged the town hall hair dyed crimson. Ira asked Clarisse about old people colouring their hair when it's obvious they'd have grey hair if they didn't, and she couldn't answer him because her face was full of maggots. Then nothing remained of her face. Eyes gone. The pool of maggots ate itself. A dog-sized maggot convulsed on the blue bed sucking up the final clots of Clarisse's blood.

Flowery light of morning pearl necklace hid behind Le Figaro splintered in his bear paws. Packed up into neat pink bags crystal earrings tight forward brow with a mean nose closed under thick cropped sandy hair and a logoed t-shirt bowling ball biceps fingers'd look good around the base of a thick cut cock. White bra smoked slow tobacco. Clouds burned draft grey by the promise of a brilliant day. Mirrors dour moustache pink headscarf on cacao skin striped headscarf on a cocoa hunchback worked the back of the bar drank pink syrup by the pint. Turbo Town's summer pulsed in afterthought. Chalet wings crusted valley walls as barnacles on a frozen hull, shells glinting razor in accelerated sun cloudless. Never take the sugar don't want to be fat or dead not good for the windows laughing hunched. Brown print fat waddled to toilet sunglasses and vests, the boff of the French vacances swept fringes and deep brown squints. None of the British redness. Accordion music cut lines through a tobacco pall ourson, then étoile and two stars. We'll be back for the skiing dans l'hiver shortest shorts tattooed lady. Ira marked out the ashtray and the hunchback signalled him to the bar with a green flash over the top of his bespectacled eyes.

Loon was here, he said. Don't move. He asked me to keep you.

Swept turbo traffic lights need I'm not the council old Intermarché don't eat the biscuit super-cycle stretched shorts showed little cocks and assholes. Glasses yellow tint threw back a baking sun. Newspaper blue room touch-live café cappuccino chocolat pedal boats on water so clean you can see the maggots seething on the bed. Too rocky for me. I have thin skin on the soles of my feet. Worked up the plants thrived on that sun dug over the beds doubly to increase maggots on Ira's leg. They sucked salt and pushed in hundreds of kilos of manure checked pH we'll need fans. Cut up the Kronenbourg red for the rude winter ourson. Special balls. There should be no cropping problem here. Corrèze wet from warming. More of a continental climate roasting summer snow for four months definitive seasons. I don't fucking believe it. Ira examined his feet, his cheeks glowing. Cadarves sucked his teeth, hooked a thumb into a back pocket.

Lulu packed the kids off to school and breathed relief. Moto helmets Ixon. I have no idea how they wear all that shit in this heat bonne journée biz. Cropped beans could never get herbs to work the cutting beams of swifts nested in the old house's eaves cheeping chicks turned their beaks as the ISS scored stars with reflected fire. The boys' first steps across filthy red tiles fell into a bearded embrace. Mud and grass everywhere, but nowhere to grow a thing. Cadarves pushed out into the oak woods. Chuck became impossible about the plastic seals in front of the road garden drunk on spring sucked up roots boys and girl pressed up against the ancient glass. Noses traced arcs over Corrèze while the deer ate down in the meadow. We can't grow anything here. It's too neat. Daffodils hard fringe switched from white to black some kind of small cheroot. Buzz cut at the bar.

I think that's the last running you'll do for a little while, said Loon, pressing his hand down on Ira's bloody shoulder. You get back on track.

Buds came up real nice in the summer and struggled in the winter. Ira absorbed the years perfected his technique exemplary hunting skills. Sanglier trapped and dead with no pain double-hard fringes brushed over maggot wouldn't leave his hand be. Ira drifted over to Loon and they lofted their cups empty in the sugar Senegal and took one each. Magic women, fifty years a piece with blonde highlights and orange tobacco residue crusting their teeth. One rotund but the other tight enough. Ira left Loon to the former double kisses red t-shirt. Loon licked his lips ran tongue tip over shark teeth adjusted white coat.

After you, he said to fatty.

Blue room of the canal burst banks. Clarisse lay dead on the floor in a pool of cold grey intestine. Lulu rubbed drying liver against the hood of her clitoris. Fatty didn't seem to mind the mess but the tight old one stuck her nose up. Lulu killed them both after Ira and Loon took turns with each then each other then with Lulu went on for weeks, but she eventually tired and strung them from the blue ceiling with the blue noose while Loon wanked them to orgasm at the point of blue death.

This isn't getting us anywhere, said Ira.

He cut them down resuscitated come-death still alive. The aged spread her labia in appreciation. Ira eased his prick in and took it out. She sucked came in orange tobacco mouth Amsterdam awash with deg. The buds flooded out of the café cellars into the canals and the street worms of deg tubes strung window streamed up from the avenues leading from Sex Town and now on the larger thoroughfares to the station sucked buds. Packs of lighters needless as the deg soaked into the water supply every cup of tea and espresso packed full of bubblegum Amsterdam dammer. Troops of blue nailed the Dutch streets, their genitals sucking up deg. Idiot bubble men fingered each other's deg asses, bluer than the Limousin sky. Stacks of windows opened from their rectums as they tumbled over and over in the deg rivers in twos then threes then fours pushed flowers behind each other's ears. A prostitute's child tapped on the window. She stood down from her plinth and opened the door to take the kid's picture and beamed, touched his cheek. Clarisse collected her organs back in lengthways and Lulu zipped her skin. Deg clouds seeped into the mairie. The mayor and his deputy, round men of questionable morals, became two of the first to succumb.

Rotterdam's trams as baffling a concept as ever devised by humans. Pespi Max avec glace lolled on one side or the other unnecessary to pay stag beetles and blue butterflies encased knocked on their glass frames behind a house constructed of windows and needles. He wouldn't allow children. Wireless headphone trance cocaine window to ease the pain. The stink of ointment to a red leather table ten thousand spiders tapped on their transparent prisons. The octopus ate coral defender of the sea trams never worked. Klaus fixed Ira onto a hole for his face straight down floor built of babies, each one of thousands sitting in a glass brick containing books and toys everything the growing child needs for healthy development. Youngsters vanished flower bricks and stars. Klaus checked with Loon permitted proceedings. He forced needles into Ira's buttocks. Ira stiffened. His cock stalactited through a hole in the table salmon tip. Klaus inserted another twenty needles and electrified them with crocodile clips fastened to a car battery.

Impressive, said Loon.

Bubbles of puss and black boils blossomed on Ira's buttocks lanced then gone, leaving silky smooth skin octopus. Loon arranged himself under the table and nibbled the head of Ira's cock. Grande moustache. Klaus greased up Ira's strong hairless ass now shaved sniffed his armpit unable to move a millimetre. Ira gasped as current mounted in the needles. Loon stretched his mouth wider and took the full head into his cheek as Klaus moved one two three four fingers into Ira's rectum and vibrated the insect walls clattered little gloved spider hands tapped the jails removed his hand cavity and waved a bottle of green poppers under his nose. The spider army pattered in glass circles hamsters on wheels generated red light through the eight-leg windows. Ira's ass clasped around Klaus's tattooed cock he ejaculated heavily into Loon's mouth as the car battery exploded. Sweet dreams are made of this. Fischer old man tipped down sunglasses and stalked the Turbo Town drag black t-shirt with two beers sucked the note. Loon tapped his ash and checked the window. Tight and fatty nowhere to be seen. A traveller with a blonde ponytail and aerodynamic cheeks gesticulated in the raw rays.

How are you able to play Ratchet & Clank if you're going away? Why won't you let me choose the song? Ira sought lines. Cologne promised to sing green bottles through the Skype window. Quick at four hours. Ira's insides smouldered from the fires of rejection a brutal sport through Luxembourg blueberry lips on the coffee cups big lemon. Biscuits frosted tables offered stale croissants. Netted windows spilled cakes and dreams. Rainbow pears adorned dirty glasses chairs with eyeless Fräuleins and carved pine hearts. A diploma from 1975 de la patisserie confiserie. The stork nests stood empty. Motivational speech to backpackers on the bandstand. A film of icing sugar stubbed Paul's white, translucent hands.

Ira drove through Luxembourg fluent German English fuck-me smile purple hair. She flipped between the two languages without blinking impeccably polite in both. Text with door code window connection details. Cup in the river leaked hordes of grey people block runners clogged the banks. Ira asked for ham in German and got chicken sausage and sauerkraut waiter wouldn't even allow him to speak the engine of Germany. Straight forward no swagger. Five on the door teenage ass so big I didn't know if it'd fit. Gay and sex two kinos. Turkish boy accordion stank deg the bikes, no panic or problem. The coffee almond didn't taste of cherries anymore watched Arsenal public smoke everywhere no problem Rusland moved the ground floor no steps up and no Cat only the bowl on the floor under the TV. James wanted to come and I sort of wish he'd been there hot streets colour love. Couples on the river under the willows as a barge inched past followed a floppy-haired sailor in Bermuda shorts. He raised his hand from the motor to light his cigarette deg slight compared to the orange bud. Guy behind the bar, cap up and round in the cheeks, said he hoped I enjoyed the weed. He turned the music down to watch the football Arsenal in the Champions League glad of the lack of combat no downside my time glad of the window to be done with work deg up doubly: beef it up. A general state of confusion uniformity drives acceptability. Sativa eleven euro a gram persistent stream of people buying buds glitched on the Arsenal window blood soaked referee's face. Soaring chest guy came in buying fags clearly wanted weed but too nervous. Said he'd come back in a minute, that he needed some tobacco first. Laughed. Everybody. Second pipe dropped off the top short but far high fifteen-minute peak finished the coffee and left. Cigarette blundered past and ordered something not too strong short grey hair black trousers white shirt glasses businessman. Black patent shoes. Stag do with drunk dressed as a bride English. Tourists packed pavements gave me a Coke bottle Esther from the can. The mother told me to sit down and drink a cup of coffee in a café. Clock rang eleven but ten Moon Mars hung between buildings on bulging pizza street. The seller in the second place, a waspish man bristling with sarcasm, projected tension but let me sniff the buds did a good job of not taking the piss too badly out of two backpackers in front of me who asked for a bomb. Third pipe in the tummy younger busier sat in the blue room in the back German motorways hotel. She asked me to stay for breakfast but I said I couldn't after first agreeing because I made as though I remembered I had to leave early in the morning. She smiled and said OK. Some of the places, especially down by the main canals, heaved with wealthy teenagers. Didn't enjoy the recording aggressive they were exactly fresh, and I doubted I'd return. Sailed longer than expected on a motorized raft young stoners bubbled the banks smoking in the golden day. Lunch-breakers ate takeaway noodles on the walls overlooking the canals. Best not to move because he's toasting bikes are lethal and don't slow down. Busy streets in the centre packed with tourists supposed to know about the hulking spidery bikes charged down the street expect people to walk on the pavements when obviously pedestrianised. A young blond man skidded to a halt and glared at a Chinaman standing in the middle of the road watching shop windows. You always had to look there. Glad I had the window with me although there was no need for something to look at this time. Lulu would love it here. Ajax in the window rippled thanking. Blacksex. Oiled tits.

SIX ····——··

Craig and Ira through the jetlag wank corner. They scuffed down
to the Banksy, jumping their bikes over the sand breasts two on
a motor I wouldn't do that myself. Welsh scared the colour of
dead blood kept up David scalped himself. By the Alyn the grass
luminous greener bounced with ladybirds. They never came.

Under the Banksy, a quarry up in the hills away from Wrexham
in the featureless space, lay a stretch of brush dense with scrub trees
and waist-high grasses brown brilliant green nasal chlorophyll. I
have your cub. Bomber twitched next to the stone bridge at the
bottom of the hill, all whisky and grey hair pulled behind liver
spot ears. Craig and Ira swung from the tree with their pants
round their ankles. Alistair wouldn't touch Ira's cock.

Hey boys. Bomber's voice all squeaky as though he'd forgotten
his oil. Flecks of dried vomit spiralled away from his brown suit
into the lime summer air. Hey boys. Give me your pants, boys.
Take your underpants off, hey.

Craig and Ira giggled and Craig said nah. Bomber wanted to
pay them he held out fifty pence. The Alyn slushed under the
bridge behind him road's a track. No civilization. Craig said nah

and left Bomber holding out the fifty pence piece, clean and shiny, as they backed away and pushed their bikes back to the Banksy to do some jumps. Jonesy in the quarry next to the estate still with the small trees don't tell the others what we used to do. They wouldn't understand. Ira dug through memories but uncovered nothing but fragments. The deg didn't help. Even the great tubes mushrooms special windows tubes but they shed no light and failed to show themselves. No shadows out from the furthest. Pontificated with the Spoonfaces on the balcony midpoint between spiral and sombrero using every spooneye to search back down the tube no legs. Nothing. Ira used his mouth to pick up the end of a cigarette from the sand on the quarry floor while Jonesy held a loose erection and he touched his cock once. The Spoonfaces remained silent as they sifted the fractured windows at the end of the tube intersected drinks on the balcony watched the bats. Ira allowed a Cat to put her arm around his shoulders.

There's nothing there, Ira, she said. We're sure. We can close the tube.

Ira cried a little and shut his eyes. The nebulae circle balcony in fixed geometry and the Spoonfaces cut the tube then released it into purple. The Cat embraced Ira and the Spoonface mixed up some mushroom soup. Ira refused to release the Cat. Growing deg wasn't going to alter that.

There's no change in the plan. Cadarves spat a tooth. And I want to know what happened in Belgium.

Tricky, as nothing happened in Belgium apart from a terrible sandwich and a conversation as fluid in French as it would have been in English. German wedges Porsches broke in fury. The temperature rose more than forty degrees across Europe and endless melting.

I get it, Ira said, taking Cadarves's transparent hand and spitting on his shining fingers. I wouldn't stop now regardless.

Hotter and hotter. No more coffee couldn't afford fresh food from the supermarkets. Taught your kids to grow potatoes? Too late for that. Cadarves led the party up into the woods around Turbo Town blocked between larger roads not as wild here as Corrèze. You said we could sleep in the forest. Crystal so blue beyond the sombrero's black took a tube clean sativa deg and scored it to release the panes folded them back on themselves to crystal capture the shade without interference the blue of Lorraine's mountains. Steel towers speared straight pines deer fearless and sweaty. Don't pass unless you're a forest worker. Over the ridges Cadarves unlocked the electrogate to Deg 1a, a beast of a plantation hidden from the cops by a magnetic mirror onto which possible to throw any image, a field colourable with mapping using the clone tool picked up a nice HD shot from flying cameras over Xonrupt matched in swell. Cop choppers saw trees. Cadarves ushered the team inside and glued the door with rotten jism.

Chicken Tommy. Fat Bill. Claymore Henry Diggins. A sentry rework of Dirty Bomber spliced up from pants DNA. The crew stood apart from Ira and Cadarves sniffed the deg.

Sensational, said Chicken.

Cadarves used the spit hand skin shimmered translucent silver bright moon. Flour smudged on the baker's apron spunk splashed against the crackling field and crystal blue. His eyes rolled dead grey intergalactic black, flashes of fusion punctuating the purple pupils. Ira was so much in love.

This is it, said Cadarves, all toothy bright. We have three million plants in this single area, and the BitCoin business is splendid.

The Tor mask is the tenth wonder, it's true.

The lady in the post office, built like a praying mantis with mandibles the size of a young buck's leg, never questioned the deg packs. She pumped them out all over Europe at ten euros a gram happy as fucking Larry. Dammer prices tubes up no one cared no one worked no one polar beared. No cops ever called and the cash returned through BitCoin exchanges into the Swiss accounts but never through US customs. It stank. Cadarves grabbed one of the deg plants round the base. The top flowers more than two metres high nice sativa over five ounces. Claymore cocked a snoop. Cadarves pulled on the stem and the roots cracked out of the plum pudding earth clodded with the best compost Corrèze banana skins smoked crack in the corner there's a mugging going on over there. A boy emerged, his skin the same flashing liquid metal as Cadarves's extraneous appendages, some fifty centimetres high with bright red wings unfolded his shimmering ruby feathers and ginger webbed toes. Arced tears scoured his cheeks then detached from his skin and vaporised, popping into violet steam. Black rimmed diffuse white eyes liquid chain links built his arms of a substance which flowed upwards towards his shoulders. His penis was very thick in relation to the size of his body and long enough to fit into his mouth which was full of rippling waves of razor metal the rows of teeth slotting in under the rim of his bell which had been reinforced with a fizzing border of frozen mercury. He trotted forward on all fours sucking the end of his own dick, chirping like a pig.

Three million, said Cadarves. The Border Boys.

Chicken Tommy had a flap.

BMW wedges on the autobahn so hot. Amsterdam Helen cooled after Ira declined her breakfast. At the far end of the leather library a smoky-eyed backpacker pretended to look at the internet.

How's the window?

Helen snorted and shuffled her crab hands. Ira ignored her and ran a finger over the browser's stiff shoulder no more than twenty, a brown crew-cut Facebook. Asian eyes misty black heard you were looking for the Border Boys. Whiteless eyes swivelled round face. Ira tweaked the wave synthesiser his cock came up real hard.

Window spent. Let's fuck.

Over the canal and up to Sex Town dream gates bikes student took Ira in mouth and lips fluttered over balls flashed bright red. Ira fucked him hard in the ass chewed on the end of his cock. He shouted, scratched at Ira's buttocks pushed into his bowel sprayed delicate violet semen into the canal and onto the rafts.

How long are you staying here? asked Loon. This isn't the show it used to be. Cold as fuck.

You're online media?

Yes. Close to cutting his fucking throat.

You can't come in.

Ira used blood as lubricant to fuck the podgy guard close to the turnstiles. Fat guard cop suit you can't come in. I will slice your throat, rub the resulting blood on my genitals and push my erect cock into a fat German man wearing police uniform stripped off his braces white underpants smeared with shit after watching the slaying of the stick-thin badge-preventer. Ira could have mistaken him for a synth faint glow of arteries and veins carrying super-conductor liquids fusion skin but blood said so. Ira shredded the guard with a bayonet, pushed the tip of the knife into his ass then sawed back and forth until his bowel prolapsed in a shower of gelatine shit and blood. Straight up into the Messe. Dankeschön.

Not the show it used to be, said Loon.

Yet again, the booth sported no internet access, so no windows hooked up to the GDC line Twitter Facebook full of games doing nothing but Reddit. Cadarves called him window. He floated green hologram ran through intersected with images of the Border Boys preparing to commit suicide on a beach the colour of volcanoes. Fragments of bulletproof glass showered scavenger hunt parquet flooring photek rarely posted pictures of full-clothed girls but this is just outstanding.

You need to chase out of Cologne, Cadarves said as the Border Boys shot themselves. Plenty more where they came from. Border Boy metal cock up bigger than a man. Cadarves lay them out on the beach: the Headless Boys. He climbed a ladder and eased his ass over a dead Border Boy cock stretched to the size of a football into colon.

I can't get out of here.

How long did it take you to come up this morning?

Five hours.

The pinched expression of disapproval. Loon sucked his teeth as if five hours was somehow a long time dead on the beach as Lulu entered full-time postal deg production. She began, as predicted, to hit it off with Cadarves had the Border Boys farming deg and seeds Ira brought back from Amsterdam squirled out real nasty. Ira squirreled away ten grams for himself and Lulu; they smoked it in the evenings up on the hills around Turbo Town watched the windows and waited for winter, jabbering and smiling through the tubes.

Let's go to Warsaw, said Lulu, but it seemed unlikely they'd find enough time. With the deg nearly done and the cold coming learned to ski jacket warm you'll need to buy some gloves, you know? So your fingers don't fall off?

Lulu put her hand, a milky spread of slender fingers, across his knee.

You shouldn't be smoking, Ira, she said. "Loon'll take you back, and there's no sense in that. I heard you coughing the other day.

Veins crowned Ira's ass cleared the deg up and for the first time he saw inhalation as a finite factor. Tubes waved permanently around both himself and Lulu. When they walked close together their tubes fused outermost allowing perusal of the annotated segments of the permanently bared fundamentals of each other's personality picked out the tougher parts the less congenial elements fed from each other's progress.

I heard you coughing.

Because you can see them, can't you my darling?

Rotund pensioner in a green floral dress strutted on stage after the fellow in the street, so thin he looked as though he'd been sucking pints of vinegar, sat next to Ira on the curb and asked him what he was doing there. Curiosity curly white hair hysteria spectacles. Knobbly hands clasped over blue rinse next to her in the mote beams stained glass. Not old enough to belong to Jesus. You can see them can't you my darling and Ira said he could even though he couldn't. Long before the Spoonfaces this, but the rinse and curly mop got a call from Barry, the dead one, after he vapoured into the gloomy church. Ira squinted at emptiness. The wine bar pine benches yellow light and the letters laid out on the table smoked deg on the cobbles whispered who's there and this time no joke: the glass span and almost crashed to the floor. The two brothers pulled white eyes spelled out flight details pills in the car park needed another. Ira slammed in a boiler suit gas mask and bobble hat first contact with the Spoons.

Instant familiarity he'd always known the Spoons and the Cats certainly his entire life red brick house. Spoons and Cats gambolled and died, stroked and scratched. The Spoonfaces arrived after ascension larger tubes cloth auras shrouded convex plastic cement cast down their circular black beady eyes. Down onto the club podiums transmitted through carbon clouds way up on the pill extension differed deg tube more of a painted mirror plastic warped reflection and declined dissection allowance instead providing a muffled view and other created black eyes and white teeth shone with the x-ray emissions of cracked convection. Spoonfaces managed the stars fields from the Balcony of Light and their war with the Cats ended long before. The Spoonfaces once hid their auras in the spreading rooms but unnecessary after sheathed claws. Starry avenues of glass and jewels replaced towering prophylactics of impossible semi-atom porticoes the days of metal cubes. Electrons broadened wider radii gave rise to the Catisk period bridges among suns clips undisruptable material capable of blocking energy through its unravelling of the molecule. Walkways along the peaks of a red giant's dwindling corona turrets, bloody in the young light of denser fields and their diamond arms. Curtains of fire hundreds of thousands of kilometres wide crashed over the sparkling shafts, over emerald passages and luxurious apartments in which mingled the Spoons and the Cats.

When are you going back?

The Spoon smoothed mud over his knees. I don't intend to remain away for very long.

Ira clogged a glass pipe with some of the Super Silver Haze he drove back from Amsterdam. Clean, if a little confused from around thirty-two degrees removed from the user. The primary problem with sativa is the rapidity of decline, although it beats being nailed to a chair. Important to get everything done by Christmas glowing chaps joined a different strain from indica roots the B-Boys. Cadarves harvested with the Borders. The second type hulks no solid surface like a gas giant push your hand straight through the entity displayed a little scorn but nothing more. Slick liquid surfaces resembled an oil rainbow, gradients of colour beaming upwards and downwards on funeral ripples fluctuating. A blue light deep within responded physically to its environment handled objects, for instance, by use of a red cellulose glove. It gave Ira the willies. Cadarves and the Borders cropped thousands of plants per day. The waters glistened around Deg1a's limits, feeding the sativas while others manipulated machines in the central areas tangerine sunsets carbon dioxide licked through the gases with the heavy formality of a night-shift nurse. Ira left early on most days to get through the forcefields in good time and back up to the Spoon midnight transfer and only thirteen euros for a return. It's really not bad and what the fuck is wrong with you?

Don't talk to me.

Next time we'll bring some water. I like the school through the window. That made me chuckle. It can't be real.

Corridors high and dull, warm paints of France ancienne. Dungarees and caps at thick angles. A train climbed in the playground. Ira didn't need to say a word.

I think it's time we went back, murmured Lulu through a moue.

Ira strolled with the Spoonfaces bevelled ruby avenues aged to star memory reflections. White windows clouded with smoke. Eyelids drooped over Cadarves's grey irises and the star nurseries melted into icy agitation. Ira took a table in the café, a bright place focused on beer, and ordered an espresso. Cadarves pocketed his change and stirred brown sugar into the tar blue spots on painted glass ten eighteen temperature. We'll both go down to the school for the first couple of weeks then take it in turns. Lulu tapped her keys dead fish crusted purple seas two heads crocodiles floated backside. Tribesmen peppered the lake's edge ladybird with oil fell on their poisoned arrows as if through syrup. Penguins ate penguins. The underside of an iceberg. The snowy edge of Remiremont. Ira shouldered open the estate agent's door and pressed his lips together as the blizzard whipped his hooded head.

I'm looking for a studio here, he said. I need a place to rent.

The cockroach licked its paws and glanced up from the coffee-stained sheets of a loose contract.

Surely, he replied in French, waving a cartilage fist. Meet me in the back.

Ira stepped out into a storage area. Loon monitored the situation via HD livefeed routed through Ira's watch. Glancing streetwise as the cockroach shuffled him into a four-wheel-drive white Audi chains on the tyres, Ira pulled his scarf tight they powered out into powder. The village's cleaner quarters flattened as he weaved into the war period high rise.

You had any problems finding it? We need to go to the cave.

Two women in their fifties. Ira assumed sisters both wore yellow floral patterns on floating blouses and shorts got away from the heat solid unemployables in new trainers smoked cigarettes under the face of a block bleached by blue winter. Banania figurines filled a plastic cupboard behind her head she opened the door down into the cellar concrete tube. Every apartment in the block had its own cave in a communal corridor spaced dead white lights encased in a wire grill for hundreds of metres. The cockroach tip-tapped behind the two women swung their backsides under the lights grisly shadow, concrete without respite. The sisters stopped outside the last door, a green safe with a padlock.

I'm losing the signal, said Loon. Get the fuck out of there.

Ira closed all windows and brushed past the older woman through the door into a desk concrete cell. She snapped the lock behind the cockroach and removed her dress. The estate agent scuttled up onto the ceiling with a series of crisp taps and lifted open his shell wide enough to form a pane then swivelled eyes back full view of cell two women now both naked didn't bother speaking French to Ira pulled down trousers cock up ridged with reversed hooks shark in spirals and the skin tough and deep and brown now more than thirty centimetres long. The women se voir the first arranged herself bushy cunt onto desk so backside stuck buttocks upwards the bare bulb's sick light cockroach ramped up to higher frequency. Her sister licked her asshole alternately spitting on Ira's cock stroking its length. She stood breasts flat against the top of her belly in front of Ira and took his cock in both hands jerked it vertically. Ira pulled his foreskin back to clear the bell. She dribbled on the tip and massaged it to a bright finish then he pushed into her sister's cunt lying on the table now asparagus flashing black air vents opened in her back bony structures spider legs became clearer as Ira inserted himself full length before pushing out with the teeth to fix himself immovable around to his backside and worked two fingers up into his ass. He squealed.

Ca c'est formidable, said the cockroach.

The humanoid on the desk completed her transformation with beating palms. The definition of the fingers vanished lumps for hands flashed green and yellow octopus her skin unstable under-surface cartilage pushed out like fingers on a deflated balloon. Hips broadened entire body now rolling with a vomitous shade head vanished into neck spine ridges two tiger yellow and black eyes dripped gelatinous liquid erupted from the top of her back and a slotted mouth replete with bleeding shattered teeth formed in resultant hole in her neck. Sister now inserted forearm into Ira's rectum knelt behind him grinning. Ira ejaculated muscles in arms tore teeth retracted.

This good for you?

Absolutely, yeah.

After the money changed hands Loon rapped on the window and demanded to be shown around. The cabin consisted of two rooms, one of which was a toilet. Only a considerate splattering of roofs and a steeple scared pine woods rolled away from the window. Lulu dropped her keys onto the desk as the sun set down in the valley.

Correct, she said.

Loon's mask kept from the electrofield never knew Ira constructed the window lattice through cellar antenna the sisters came every week stocked cupboards with glass jars of peaches and plums in syrup. Lulu brought boys up to the cabin sometimes with Ira and sometimes not. They fucked on the floor while Ira pushed pins into the sides of his head to better maintain contact with the square construction. It took two knitting needles. He used his toolkit to attach and dial direct into the router, pushing the tips into the centre of his eyes. Thin oyster liquid ran down the needles and connected with the window network further through the optic nerve Lulu fucked on the bare floor, teen spunk gluing her ass pounded on thick French balls on her cooldown but not be for long. Ira withdrew the needles and the cockroach patched him up.

I need to play.

Lulu sat with her back to the bar using the window as a mirror.

Him, she said.

Dark buzz-cut endurance sports build no fat cut up nicely large arms we'll have to think about this. Lulu reached under the table and unzipped his fly flopped tooth cock fell semi-erect against the top of his jeans. She roughly pinched the glans, impassively slapped it, knocked his dick backwards and forwards. She sighed and masturbated him with a gloved hand until he ejaculated onto the underside of the tabletop where the semen stuck like wallpaper paste and looped down onto the floor careful not the get any on the glove sneered at Ira and signalled the runner left the table to join him at the varnished bar.

They chatted briefly and the light dimmed in the car but Ira kept the engine running. He kissed her neck in the rear-view mirror lit a cigarette when he inhaled and turned they'd vanished. He blew smoke through the window and clutched to first, crunching out over ice. They'll be back later sure blew in while working through the back half of his article, the pines in the background flawless silhouette against a belligerent smear of sunset. Ira invited the runner inside with a condescending smile clearly freaked out didn't bother to hide the deg or hypos. Lulu lounged drunk. Stick it in my leg. Yellow sapins obsidian windows not a soul for half a kilometre. The athlete got a little carried away with Lulu the inside of the chalet varnished a deep white sat on a bench heart cut through the back. Ira offered a tumbler of red wine, and he finished it in a gulp before thumping the Swiss glass on the wooden floor. Lulu rotated her hips opposite Ira perched on his edge of his desk. She touched the heel of one black boot to the toe of the other.

So, said Lulu.

Je ne parle pas anglais, he said confusion smoothing his smile as Ira rose away from the desk produced a blue-painted crowbar and arced its hooked end into the top of crew-cut's head. His skull fractured with the sound of snapped wood. Lulu's nipples dimpled her dotted dress his arms draw pink trails in the polished chalet air and he started to fit. Ira threw down another strike, this one exposing the brain. He stopped at that. Crew-cut writhed on the rug head holes fountain blood already declining with pressure loss. Taut mouth Ira dropped the dripping bar bounced on a green cushion canapé, bulb-light glancing from his fatless arms.

So, said Lulu.

It took some fearsome time to soak him down. They zipped him into a building sack his body refused to adopt an easy angle as Ira heaved him from the chalet to the boot of his car.

What about Loon?

Fuck him and the pigboys, Ira said as he started the engine. Windows off.

Hardly. Loon prowled valley interspace and took in the whole show called Ira trans-window the following day and ordered him into the surgery.

And what the fuck was that, exactly?

Ira picked his nails. He had to go. It was important.

You'd better be ready, Ira.

Lulu says I will be. Stop worrying so much. Come for dinner next week.

Loon chewed the inside of his cheek and reclined into black leather office chair brave winter sunlight slanting through the blinds. Ira cursed his ill-fitting sunglasses. Sydney, and many mistakes. That money belongs to Sarah boiled eggs in a kettle made of a single piece not possible to open it. Fucking poms. Fishing rod red flaking paint. I can't believe you've never done that luminous mackerel from the end of Brighton Marina paid the warden by the rod. Captain Cadarves. White sweater in the winter Channel spray pay me respect black as dogs out past the lighthouse didn't catch anything for three weeks. He held the fish down on the bleached pier boards and collapses its skull with the line's lead weight. Ira took it home and fried it in olive oil on the verge of retching over the smell of worms on his fingers. The fish tasted nice though plenty of mackerel after that. They judged him with their dead eyes and flapped in the Tesco bags the Sainsbury's bags pressed their bloody faces against the plastic gasped for an air they couldn't breathe while bandage clouds dressed the torn lighthouse foam arched over the embattled mole. Ships alternated starry green and blue cranes and lemon dolls for lifting the nets dirty yellow spotlights died on the water trawled the weed-strangled, bomb crater waves.

Yachts in the locks.

Piano tilted on the grey beach stone and café crowns gleamless on the front. A cosy fire. Didn't hit it off. Desperate singing in a fresh-paint living room text after we left then vanished. Mother's group in the church the vicar took Ira by the arm and threatened him over Lulu very upset. She leapt up from her seat ate sandwiches in the car before whisking them back to Germany.

Crew-cut stopped flapping. Lulu smoked and Ira draped a hand over her shoulder, his chest pressed against the blue t-shirt. The plan didn't seem to matter anymore.

Take care, Ira called up the slope to the little girl. The Vézère lay at the bottom of a valley so steep it hurt his knees weight of the pack on his back rested next to trees moved her from one place to the other with concentration.

Don't fall, sweetheart.

At the base of the gorge Ira tutted and refreshed the window. No signal dinosaurs still light enough to push on, but no point returning. It's fine. Just get on with it. Ira practised his knots and had the bivouac up in five minutes. The mats and sleeping bags curled in the dusk. He checked his combat knife and armed the child, mindful of the Glock in his backpack. They camped right next to the river, the water burbling in the moonlight stand next to a tree. Embrace bark in the dying light, alone in a place no one would ever want to go, completely alone, and watch the summer's day vanish. Listen to the leaves giggle in the beeches and allow the bats to decorate the air around your head. Cook canned sausages and lentils on a gaz stove noodles sweet bread and bottles of water. Ira broke down the shelter and packed the sheeting away while the girl kicked her shoes on a rock and studied the river. He slid the clip from the pistol and tapped the accessible round, then ensured the knife lay within easy reach. They'd arranged to meet Lulu at seven and couldn't be late no signal didn't want her to worry.

But the window always there black links and blue links and red links check it. Check the account the UK account French account business account shut the UK account US has cracked the BC matter of time until the drones decoded the tree cover on Deg 1a. Cadarves picked his nose.

Come with me, he said, flicking a wet bogey.

Up now. Come on, love. We have to meet mummy. Straight-up power-drums for Friday. Cadarves slotted GPS into his abdomen skin passed over leaving a seven-inch screen shining through translucent radiating out into the pines beyond the saplings the hunters used to mask their hide. New smell of resin baited the deer out onto the needle-soaked cliffs. Illusion air between the trunks Cadarves floated his boots skimmed the needles a milky field GPS automated foot movement. Ira tied his laces Kiefer Sutherland super-distracting Xbox One window ad no games attention-seeking emo girl had back to school inspired bassline ruder than Iranian pornography. War is hell. The field fractured as Cadarves approached, Ira holding back, and then vanished to reveal a ten-kilometre Vosgienne valley wall of purple deg buds as thick as Ira's arm, flowers so dense they dragged the branches to the earth. Cat stench escaped the open field. Ira crossed and the gate shuddered invisible behind him to replace the space between the pines with more pines get something on the board. We didn't see anything last month. Ira struggled to quell panic.

You should stop worrying, said Cadarves. We're moving the internal culture to a yearly view. This is the main event.

Need to push up to a thousand and drank coffee in the Turbo Town cafés every morning don't help. The buds up in Deg2a shone a phosphorescent purple to the horizon. Tons of deg to give those Parisian Border Boys something to think about. Ira's tubes flapped around his head galvanistic tentacles as he trailed Cadarves drifted across the plantation reflected back from the mirror shield NRA hadn't cracked any of this year and Deg 1a nearly cropped problem with week days so many windows followed both Ira and Cadarves through Deg 2a mapped heat signatures and scent displays through metal balaclavas replaced fields like the second boys impossible to physically damage him through vapour skin. Cadarves stroked the buds as he sailed past, the thunder drums trichomes sticking to his clacking bony fingers thick white jumper shed GPS red lines through the bud fields forever sketched shapes Sat8 could map from space and out interstellar.

Does Lulu know about this?

Lulu knows about everything, Loon said, shaving his upper lip.

Down by the bridge elongated sprites with no genitals ridges up their backs, blind white, no hair, jade green eyes, loitered behind rocks as the children played hairy giant sluiced upstream. He paused to inhale water through his nose and scattered the diamond fairies. The children fled. Quartz moss converted the rocks to salmon pink, lustrous in the rising sun. The ridgebacks regrouped after the ogre made his way further up the muddy river but the children didn't return. A clutch of queens merged white glue flecked with bones crept over granite stripped them of hard lichens. The frost worked through Deg2a's outer edges purpling then depositing bricks of deg bud. Tubes bloomed from the glue pancake like mushrooms wet log. Larger sets of windows built out the worm-heads, exploding and coagulating under the sky field's fluctuating areas. Charlie. Charlie, help me. Everybody dies. Buzz-saws in the pines. Bee-saws in the forest threw trunks into the tooth trucks stripped back they won't come this far up.

We're ready for operation, said Cadarves.

Closeted beside the périphérique, Cadarves and Ira fucked with Lulu in the back of the matt van. Lulu hacked them both with an axe before eating Ira's shrunken brain. She chopped Cadarves's legs at the knee he choked on blood punched his chest until the skin split and she was able to remove the GPS screen pushed it into Ira's head to reformat the neurons. Everybody's dead buzz-saw white queens separated themselves from the rest of the group shot through cassis ice cream. Clichy-sous-Bois crumbled into the weir as Ira, Lulu and Cadarves floated over the kerbs on trailing deg tubes. Lulu strapped canisters of deg juice to their backs and THC direct into assholes. Cadarves snapped the scientist's neck and fed his assline into the reservoir will take many hours pumped in deg levels high enough to raise tubes on La Chêne Pointu sewer flowed purple we'll need some dye. We have plenty brought in the white fairies: they flowed into the cleansing plant separated shed out residue into the reservoir then sank beneath the dam's surface a tube left clear drinker brimming with THC. Klout moment sign in with Twitter. I'm obsessed with Sharon Osbourne's face. I don't fucking care I'm in twat mode. It's a twat day. Can you cover the book? She says she doesn't want to do it. What the fuck? It'll cost a fortune if we have to do it ourselves.

Cello in the bushes. Vite. Allez-y. I'm coming tomorrow but I'm not going to tell you at what time because I'm a fucking cunt. Don't stop and don't watch the clock or this isn't going to work white on black unable to pass on the street I don't know what the fuck he wants to talk about. You can't do that until you're seven, and I don't want to hear another word stop piling more on the bed. Like a hotel. Lulu touched Ira but out on a deg tube and wouldn't entertain it. I don't see the point in having sex anymore, not after what we've been through. I don't believe you and that isn't especially charitable. Don't stop. Water on mirrors. Metal in the winter sun. Mauveine lake waves no filter. There's a foreign language section but there hasn't been much use for it until now. I'm going to look at the board. There's nothing there. What the fuck am I going to do about my French? I could call Charlene and do it over Skype but I doubt that'll work. There's this man here, a young fellow looks fresh. I'll call him for you if you like. Ira clouded off in the spluttering 911.

The teacher answered after three rings. Oui allo?

Lulu trotted out some formal French instructing him to come to the chalet at six that evening. He shuffled in, codpiecing his groin with a knitted green bobble hat. Ira wrote at the desk. Lulu stirred pasta. She shifted the matelas over to the far wall before inviting him in and kissed him through pillar box lipstick. Ira sparked a joint. The kid, he guessed, was no more than twenty-three burgled scum insurance companies forgot the police. A side-parting sharpened under the chandelier some kind of product coated piano hair smoothed back and not a strand out of place white shirt top button unfastened and tan brogues. Shit suit. Ira blew a smoke ring and passed the joint over to the teacher while Lulu cleared her throat and offered up English tea. The younger man fingered the smoke and drew, exhaling through his nose a slender deg tube snaked from his neck the windows evenly spaced wrapped round entered the back of his head then through the central part of his face fractured eyes spider the tube settled over his scalp in a crystal rose candied with gold. He handed the joint back to Ira, who took his time over his next draw.

So, said Ira.

My name is Regis, Regis slurred in English before producing his own deg. Ira flicked a red lighter and flamed the end of the joint deg pure tricky to smoke. Lulu poured some milk into Regis's tea while he loaded a small bong with a mixture of deg and white powder. Lulu and Ira stripped off. Regis blew up the rainbow stars the Spoonfaces through the wall behind Regis's head and floated reversed through Lulu turned their backs on the three and exited through the roof cheetah watched vita light kindling cars matched calculator bar red shotgun speaker monitor Lulu spread bodily sliced rock out fanned Ira tried to grab Regis's cock missed again succeeded sucked seed. Regis fucked Ira's face deg tubes thrashed netted octopi thousands of deg windows splintered as Lulu collected enough of herself to move Ira's face sat on Regis's cock first pussy then ass allowed Regis to ejaculate anal then Ira sucked it out frogspawn glue flash room glowed brighter than the Cat walkway showered semen skin redness in check mottled Ira turned Regis over inserted table leg into ass fucked mouth removed furniture smashed him beat him so hard he tore a bicep while Lulu pushed her fingers into her ass to coat them with Regis's semen and Ira's saliva then used them lubricated to massage clit to orgasm as Regis screamed ribs crunched lungs collapsed blood welled from his lips squeezed through teeth his head split inside muscle fat bone Ira punched the top of his head away from his upper jaw and inserted his fist into his throat thrashed on the end of his wrist skin green chopped his limbs with a boning knife and bow-saw he bought at Treignac brico for a fiver. Lulu paraded through Turbo Town with a feather duster gelato road surface awash with globular semen and blood pumped from the space where Regis's head used to be exploded bought Lulu a Grimbergen still stood in the restaurant itself. Ira couldn't settle and stabbed Regis in the scrotum with a steak knife held him against the bar by the throat yelled unable to move his Adam's apple vertically because of the pressure on his neck yeah, fucking do it, cut my fucking balls off, stick the knife up my fucking ass, make a hole in my fucking neck and fuck it, you fucking brute, so Ira did although he didn't exactly curry favour with the restaurant's management. They asked Ira and Lulu to leave, and then told them to return to clear up the mess.

He's in no fit state to do it himself, said the maître d'hôtel.

Red fruit freckled the far side of the ditch and the clouds propped restless on the ski jump mountains. Neva and Jami skirted the bottom of the single-pane freeze in the winter someone there in the summer bilberry floated on a bubble of silver gas and Jami transported by thought. White dust sheets shrouded the living room empty the garden log pile cream past its sell-by. Neva streaked up into the clouds and Jami matched her at short intervals over the pine forest through Xonrupt Longemer to monitor Deg3b and Sat8j, hovering out over the steepest of the passes between Gérardmer and Munster. The water population harvested trillions of plants, green reeds in the shallow end full wetsuits and shoes couldn't see some fucking prick with an umbrella, the young black seal powering through the pool wheels slapped the boards hooted bells bass balsamic on my Nike FuelBand. Acriflavine eyes laced with victory red carpet glass rainbow thumped vomit through the policeman's face.

Vite, he said, wiping crimson lumps.

Neva banished the cop and atomised his gun while Jami vanished into his legal asshole muck-spreaded the young turbos with brown gore. Why hasn't he come round yet? What's his fucking problem? Two hard motherfuckers opened a deg tube without Ira found it increasingly difficult needed to up the dose Cadarves stroked his thigh. I saw Jami earlier I don't believe you. Cadarves loaded the cop's pistol pulled on the GIGN uniform and stomped from the van. Lulu dragged the hat over her eyes, a chipolata joint slapping the window out on the street boots crunched before the estate's sheer face. He brandished the dead gun in a series of heavy clicks. Black men smoked cigarettes against a wall Cadarves warned the largest under arrest told him to go fuck himself raised the muzzle and shot him in the neck slammed against breezeblocks in red star Cadarves shot the next man in the balls while the third escaped cigarette span in the air Parisian water deg content critical water supply saturated. Lulu exited vehicle naked apart from the blue hat injected THC into her cunt. Ira's balls swelled football pink after their dose upped deg tubes streamed self-ingested lucent volcanoes. Lulu howled topaz eyes extended in plate-sized ovals on stalks from her forehead tubes massed around her cracked, polychromatic face lifted elephant crushed of windows fractured the image sparked lines of information fused head split open eyes clicked unlinked chameleon disassembled Paris sub-atomic grid. She removed gas supplies revolved concrete into carbon variant hydrogen and converted tenth arrondissement to reflective cube wave separate human. Lulu tubes muscular hunched over Ira Cadarves estate launched broadside against massing police arranged communications spin from the surfaces of the Enclos-St-Laurent edifice concentrated deg beams sliced two satellites into a shower of vacuum snow. Neva and Jami sucked up orbital debris directed back down in city-wide scramble beam cars Molotovs drew flaming arches through the putrid Paris after-sun. Cadarves out of his uniform naked Lulu administered THC suppository glass sabre-tooth shoulders crowded police fatalities as the estates advanced on the Paris centre they will try to sell you climate change and you mustn't submit: the only way is no way sun stripped the bare earth even barer.

Jami's heat shield, forged by the Cats, was capable of the desert sand long devoid of human life impossible to remove energy produced by the body at rest. My father taught me how to survive in the woods, taught me how to trap a deer and find a boar, taught me how to kill a pig and clean a gun. He taught me to read English. I can speak three languages Lulu German. Jill pulled her head down behind the rock. She stunk up level and took a speculative shot at the middle-aged primary school teacher crawling through the undergrowth beneath her close enough to remove her leg with the twelve-gauge. She didn't even scream. Jill dropped down and sucked the blood from the wound flooded the forest path. She stabbed her neck cried mercury tears then butchered her in the shelter wrapped her limbs in polythene and dangled them into the river tied to overhanging trees to keep them fresh washed the blood from her mouth.

I'm sorry, she said.

She replaced the spent cartridge and examined the weapon.

Oil-bright shined from the surface of the teacher's Colt magnum came fully loaded. She stuck to the deer never came down too steep built the bivouac in less than five minutes slices of dried buck nearly a month old ribs threatened to tear out from gossamer skin dug in the ground with her Ka-bar scratched for grubs found a dead rat cooked it on a fire built from fallen leaves and ruined, oily jeans. Paris trees grew up through the cracks. A crumbling parapet shielded as she crouched separated high tenement slates and oiled the pistol. She patted the knife in her pocket a light and a torch just as her father showed her kill never hesitate you cannot hesitate kill anyone everyone. Under the growth cube the Champs-Élysées tarmac no longer visible floated out to the north satellite rays bounced from its rotating surfaces lit patches of the city in white death. Pistol to chest tapped the Ka-bar chanced a look: streak of moss bubbling white clouds spat. My father taught me how to survive in the woods, to build the fire in a depression no one can see the flames unless they're overhead. An old Vietnam trick for signalling choppers without getting shelled on the LZ.

Sea of green.

Lulu checked the account to find little left after the new furniture and clothes we had to buy the bed and the mattress and the other bed and we have to have coats because of where we live. Ira couldn't disagree. Moved some money over you don't live in one of the tax exemption zones and you really should have consulted me before making the move. You have three children. The deg channel widened and I don't see a serious problem with the site managed the transition. Everything's going to be fine. Get a large. Un café, s'il vous plait. C'est moi signed up for a French course, a year-long foundation provided free by the French government. Hollande's France embraced those of the correct nationality. Turkish, a lot of Turks, Albanians, Moroccans and many more countries represented here, although I should tell you that the classes are mainly inhabited by women.

That's fine, said Lulu. He likes women.

Where to go? The beasts silvered down the chalet monster up. Horns in the ass that last one didn't come up to much. I only fucked him three times before he stopped breathing.

You need to go easier on them, said Ira. Make them live through it. There's no point otherwise.

Sunlight glinted from a smiling tooth white under fathomless black of shapeshifting sunglasses strangled fantôme when it went for my daughter, pulled it to the side barely solid in my hands slipped through my palms like trying to grab hold of jelly in a swimming pool. Off into the shadows of her room it gibbered, laughed hysterically, made puppy noises as I pushed down on its throat felt the roped tendons in its insubstantial neck punched it in the face punched it punched it until it could only twitch unable to stand kicked it to death against the radiator, reached into its chest and tore its lungs out it cried dead. The girl slept fitfully under a window full of stars and snow. I stroked her fringe to one side and kissed her forehead.

Lulu skidded and twisted her leg underneath her backside remained unbroken.

The mairie's entrance hall, a slim room of egg paintings and historical photographs of French farms, flinched from its dusty laze as Cadarves pushed through the council pine door and wiped greasy fingers over the hip of his jeans. The woman behind the counter touched her ear pink spectacles and organised a date to visit the chalet. She arrived blue nude from the snow placed her glasses on the counter unzipped Cadarves's trousers and sucked his cock. Lulu knelt beside her in a pair of blue shorts and a black bra. The mairie assistant removed Cadarves's cock from her mouth and pushed it between Lulu's lips swung her head back and forth cupped Cadarves's shaved, angular balls. Mairie woman (let's call her Louise) bit the shaft of his cock while Lulu sucked hard on the tip. Cadarves pointed to the sofa and Louise sat opened her legs. Lulu fingered her cunt licked her clit. Cadarves stepped over her shoulder and she took his cock back into her mouth started to moan as Lulu lapped at her cunt then used fluid from her labia to lubricate her puckered asshole and slid one then two fingers into her rectum. Louise rubbed her own clit while Lulu fingered her ass, squeezing the hood between her ring and index fingers. Cadarves pulled his cock from her mouth and she opened her lips wide wanked him onto her tongue, thick jets of semen over her lips dripped down to her tits inserted a third finger into her ass and Louise came wanking hard on Cadarves's cock while Lulu nibbled her clit and thumped three fingers in and out of her ass.

Next.

A Turkish man fucked Ira cock pierced through the urethra with a weighted silver horseshoe could feel it high up in his bowel. His anus stretched tight over the base of his cock while he gently screwed him, his buttocks shaking with each slap of hip. Steak pecs. He held him steady around the waist three other men stood to his side wanked touched each other's dicks occasionally spoke words of encouragement to the Turk pumped iron slapped his ass built slowly to climax. Ira pushed his cheek down onto the desk grabbed his own semi-erect cock but every time he tried to start wanking himself the Turk slapped his hand away gentle fucking high up in the bowel. The other three well-built and blond American yeah go on fuck him yeah the Turk approached to a slow orgasm then controlled himself so as not to damage Ira's rectum when he finally came bit his bottom lip eased his piercing from his ass slathered in semen the other three rock hard as he withdrew the Turk stepped aside and the first blond, a head taller than the Turk, lifted Ira's hips and slid his thin long dick up his ass. Ira motioned the Turk around to his face while the American accelerated his strokes, the Turk's semen coating the length of his cock welling around his anus. The Turk moved to Ira's mouth licked the semen from the length of his softening dick while the American grunted and approached ejaculation. The Turk stiffened again the room glowed gold the other two Americans couldn't wait any longer. The larger of the two led the other to the bay windows and positioned his leg up on a quilted velvet red chair clear access to rim his little pink asshole. He licked it good and wet slapped the top of his prick. Legs up behind the ears penetrated and came almost immediately pulled himself out and sucked the come out of him then allowed him to rim back and fucked his ass until he came again. Ira spurted and passed out. The Turk left in a hurry.

New suit. Maybe you'll need two of them, and it's important to realise there's a difference between American and British English. There are other forms, obviously, but those are the two primary not just a case of removing u from everything Australians have a tendency to add 'o' to the end of nouns. You buy beer at the bottleo, for example, and Tom becomes Tommo. The target language especially important when working across business assignments far too expensive here and I certainly wouldn't pay ten euros for half a piece of cheese. It can't possibly have cost four euros to send a postcard urge to kill. Ira tried his best to keep Lulu in check but he wasn't as young as he used to be. Come on my face like being sprayed better than just swallowing everything fuck my ass harder, for fuck's sake. She left for the chemist bar theme threw cow skins and old skis wood burner wire-haired dog called Max beer probably cost four quid played some kind of bingo drank lager waited for the children to finish school once in bed she traipsed around Turbo Town in black spikes, scraping heels along the icy sidewalks. Can you do me a favour? A leather belt and long coat invited teenager to fuck her behind the linen factory refused to allow him near her cunt only in the ass using spit as lubricant and no condom she wanked him into her mouth then spat his semen over his balls slapped his dick hard recoiled in shock and walked away wiped her mouth, gathering her coat around her in the snow while he wrestled with sports underwear in a dull press of streetlights. Back at the house she removed her clothes made Ira eat her ass she tasted of shit and salt then pushed needles through his nipples clamped his cock in a vice in the basement towered next to him with a hammer wiped blood from his nipples onto the end of his distended cock tapped the hammer on the workbench he came in the prison. She ordered him to a Strasbourg piercing parlour. Ira maintained silence as the assistant pierced the hood of her clitoris got the idea and left them alone closed the door behind her told Lulu that she mustn't have sex or have oral sex performed on her without the use of a condom or some other barrier until the piercing healed. Lulu nodded and the assistant left. Lulu pushed her ass back up on the blue paper roll with her legs open and touched her tits removed a tiger-striped dildo from her bag. She sucked it. Ira hard in his jeans but refused to expose his cock in case the assistant came back then didn't care and unzipped his fly massaged the end of his cock a deep purple glistened with pre-come. Lulu coated the dildo in saliva and turned her leg over so her ass faced the camera clear view of her asshole Ira pushed her buttock up stretched she stroked the tip of the dildo inside relaxed her rectum then inserted four inches of plastic into her ass gasped slid the dildo in and out further. Ira shuffled round to the other side of the table cock heavy she took as much of his cock into her mouth while pushing the dildo as far into her rectum as possible. Ira held Lulu's head and fucked her face she grabbed his scrotum and stretched to its limit her head back opened her mouth and told Ira to come on her tongue. He ejaculated all over her face and neck, over her tongue and teeth. Lulu grabbed his cock and chewed the tip until the assistant returned.

We're going for a walk remove the filters. The little fisherman in Munster nearly crashed into a car ran up from Basel flashed his light truck lanes onto the Swiss border my dark-haired Swiss boy met me at the gate and asked why I'd come. I told him I wanted to see the airport, but he waved a hand plenty of time for that. Straight, bi, single, GSOH. Basel thick with cupids and bars flowed casual sex Lulu advanced upon another period of activity but Ira spent more time with the road-worker in Basel, fucking his ass cock hard in his stretched rectum the dark guard fluttered and his skin became diaphanous revealed his organs cock held firm in rectal walls clock said cuckoo green sticker thirteen Swiss tax wooden shop up from the valley too tired to do anything now. The certificate waited in the post. Ticked one of the final boxes. Time to turn the heating on and veal kidneys in mustard, blueberry tarts and coffee. Cod and rice. The library on Saturday morning ten o'clock for a story read by a shy French lady in the backroom children's section. Sentenced to death brother save us. The castle suspended the metal whale. The carousel. Too many accidents Newcastle or London Lulu got her German out proud. Too tired to do anything. Too tired to do anything but sleep. Checked the post and locked the car. Leave your coat there, why don't you. You think about it far too much. Just move forward at the fastest possible speed. Out and away from the dilapidated stone walls, la Vallée de Munster unfurled from the emerald fractals brown white transhuman cows as if sprouting from the pre-logical well at the portal of the protector of time.

SEVEN ———

It isn't large enough, said Ira as he tossed the screen aside. There's too much sharp.

Young couples packed the train to London with airy conversation salami pizza and a Macbooker with lank brown hair up near the ceiling pointed shoes attempted to engage Ira in talk on the plastic food's quality. Ira pretended he couldn't speak French, muttered au revoir and returned to his seat. The traveller wiped tomato from thin lips with the pads of a thumb and index finger and avoided Ira's eye as he passed. Ira pushed himself into the silver screen. No deg on those trains came into contact with the police, their fat blue dogs sniffing it out. Ira shut the laptop couldn't connect the window small screen reception gone in the tunnel went to find him in the carriage behind.

Je suis désolé, Il a dit. Le pizza était vachement bien, c'est vrai. Tu veux me baisser?

His milky wet eyes rose grey screen, his flopping fringe framing sharp cheeks. Denim, stretched over Ira's erection, twitched at a light brush of fingertips. Ira took his hand pallid skin eyes dripped milk and led him to the toilet in the red spaces between the carriages, the tunnel chewing past in the undersea dead night. Occasional sick lamp shut the toilet door. The man blabbered again about the pizza: Ira sat him on the toilet and ordered him to shit it out. Thierry shat the pizza and Ira ate it, smearing it around his mouth and then Thierry's mouth after he fished it from the toilet's metal plate flushed then cleaned them both with the sink's tiny trickle of water from deadlight washed them both no traces of shit on their hands or faces then demanded Thierry suck his cock until he ejaculated onto the back of his throat pinched Thierry's nose closed and forced his penis down until he vomited, a tide of lumps covering his scrotum and the base of his cock. Distressed jeans black ribbed socks and brown leather shoes. Ira pulled his penis from Thierry's mouth water to clean took a tissue from the pocket of his wet jeans and wiped away his French lover's pearly tears. They embraced skin melted into a single suit milky cried Ira bent over the sink and Thierry pushed his cock up into his ass his face into the mirror window slapped ass while he fucked it ground Ira's teeth into the mirrored window glass fucked him fucked him slapped his ass left hand prints on his buttocks balls slapped against the rim of his rectum then both came in a wave melt skin milky tears opened the laptop tunnel blackness soothed away to a ripple of sludgy cloud and the remaining greenery of the English countryside. Ira waved to Thierry as he departed the train at St Pancras, but the Frenchman appeared to be in some physical difficulty and required assistance from a police officer. She tapped her nightstick against a gloved palm.

Developer on screen Earl's Court stalked TV presenter trying to get the shot purple jacket like a clown. She barked at the cameraman shadows fell over her cracked late-forties face. Ira offered himself up but she didn't see him. Just the screens.

Time to push on, said Ira scheduled a time to drink coffee with Loon.

Thousands of youngsters in torn jeans and unprofessional piercings squashed their faces into the glass. The windows reached out to grab their heads liquid glass fingers pushed under the skin at the back of cheek bones the windows sucked onto their faces crushed into their eyes thousands of cosplaying emo students writhed on the carpeted floor of Earl's Court mercury screens compacting their upper faces, fountains of blood emptying over the floor and their chests and genitals. Once process complete, each one of more than fifty thousand lay flattened reformed so the area above the top lip up to the hairline had been flattened into a rectangle living liquid layer of electrified crystal. Ecstatic youngsters brain segmentation rose from the carpet soaked in gore behind the crystal compressed eyes twitched in a sealed bath of nerves electrical connections blood and brain tissue they leapt to their feet and screens irradiated with yellow and blue pulsed light brain hardwire into connection windows followed in streams conjoined with those in proximity resulting in a window network plastic glass looped tunnels connected entire crowd of stymied aspirants eyes flat twitched behind cognizant glass.

Engage the stream, said Loon. He snapped a pink rubber glove.

Olive currents speared two-dimensional eyes shot back from the windows straight into the optic nerve accessed brain centres pumped separate images. Ira stepped aside from the bloody screen faces as they staggered against each other and the pods from whence the windows originated attached dribbled blood pipe in offset stream images of gardens and stars. Hands out bumped through window arches detached and connected with the exposition centre roof beamed out impressions to a satellite back into window looped queues of begging sub-forties waiting for their chance to have their faces flattened crossed London and down into tubes around the cafés. I'd like to talk to you about marketing. Ira laughed by way of apology.

Sure, said the fat starter-upper as he skirted a painted lady windmilled naked bloody arms squealed with delight as blood pissed from her face and window flashed bright yellow powered electric duo-alien porn directly into her brain. She collapsed to the carpet, masturbating as if grating emmental. Fatty cabrioled over her with a retch.

We've captured this audience, said Ira.

I can see that. We can do it, but I want a tester. Free pipes for a month, straight into her ass.

You drive a hard bargain, said Ira.

Loon exhaled cigarette smoke. We need to move extra-screen. You fix up the meetings.

Down on the lakeside Chicken tried without success to avoid smatterings of dogshit the Russians ensconced in Paris. Circle round and we'll take a look. Scope them out. I doubt they'll be straight, said Loon, smearing his finger through the thickest end of an MDMA wrap.

The Russians bullied the entrance of the Pole Club, a venue close to Opera frequented by bitter degenerates. Ira and Loon cruised with Billy the Chimp, fresh from his Brazilian jaunt. Still pissed he wasn't included in the final trip, Ira shot Loon evils as he munched the rest of the powder and packed a deg pipe in the back of the red Citroën. Billy ticked behind the wheel, jabbering like a crackhead about his running achievements, about how what goes on tour stays on tour and Brazilian cock sizes. Loon forced one of the special pills into his mouth kept him quiet for a little while, the streetlights painting amber strips across his shining eyes. The Russians vanished on the next pass and Billy dented bumpers to park. Club women consisting only of legs. Tiny windows, each beaming silver alien pornography to flat-screener brains speckled leg platforms flat skin. Loon threw a loaf of bread but none of them noticed too busy wanking to the legs around bloody corkscrews blur speed. The Russians conspicuous by their lack of face window the rest two-dimensional eyes crushed and blurred behind pulsing porn glass slouched in the corner wore serious expressions and white suits.

You watch that fucker, Loon ordered Ira, motioning to the boss. Billy giggled and sniffed his ass. The Russian slapped him round the back of the head.

Privet, said the chief, a hulking chest with aubergine skin and match-strike stubble. He fondled his cock, an appendage thicker, longer and pinker than an Alsacienne frankfurter. Billy bent to suck it. Loon took a plush seat and Ira grimaced the leg platforms kicked sharp boots out around the corkscrews, the middle-aged men fingering each other's asses as blood spattered their faces and the silver porn stepped up from savage sadomasochism to donkey-fucking. Eyes split behind the screens marketers tore the cocks off wailed in time to the Mexican marching band. Ira smoked the rest of his bowl and ascended the deg tube positioned himself at Loon's shoulder stood over Billy came in his mouth. Billy scampered off to fuck the bleeding cock-hole of a dying conference attendee.

Spasibo, said Loon, accepting a stained sugar cube. I doubt this will end well. Ira dropped a piece with the three Russians straight out eyes bushes. We need to go tech, Russian.

And I need some ass, said the Russian. Ass first tech later. Get me some ass.

DEG   133

She smiled at him on the second pass but Ira left it too late and he never saw her again. Firm in the ass area good for the Russian. Boy ass girl ass not sure if there's too much difference but the boy ass needs plucking. Girls don't tend to need ass wax ass lick eat my ass are you sure you should be eating my ass? I really don't see why not three fingers inside her rectum. She yanked down on his scrotum with the intention to tear as he pumped three-day-old semen onto her tongue she licked it clean pushed eight inches up to the base her ass twitched next to his balls girl ass boy ass can be tighter especially if the boy ass virgin girls seldom are these days. Wank in piss toilet an upward distortion of Schipol stacked up a second thanks man you have a good evening well goodbye man got any gauzes bring sugar cubes not spending the night looking at you. Licked balls carefully wrapped end of prick lard you really hurt my ass bowel movement would you like a cup of tea. There is such a thing as common decency. The judge slammed his gavel down. The ship pulled upright. Dozens killed.

Moscow hungry but that would have to wait, and you'll have to walk to the dentist. Loon experienced difficulties of varying degrees, having mounted Billy who wore an alarmed expression as he fucked his ass with his giant purple cock slapped his buttocks with both hands roared like a tiger the Russians spiralled on the floor laughed uncontrollably. Loon juggled bread circle round leg platforms tiger man scratched the stage with his stilettos. Conference men now ate each other's dismembered cocks and Ira pulled Loon, Billy and the Russians through the door to the waiting cab as the turbo police stormed the building.

Thanks, said Loon, whacking Billy around the chops with the end of his spunky dick. Paris at night drifted by. The Russians got into some bad anal play in the back of the taxi while Loon cleaned himself up kissed Billy mopped the milky tears. Even Ira winced Russian number three did not appear to be having a good evening was probably dead before they got into the car. Loon helped the two Russians, the biggest two, heave him out of the taxi door and slammed it shut blocked out the rainy Parisian streets. His hardening corpse bounced along the tarmac shed skin and muscle.

Food for thought, said the Russian.

Loon called Ira a prick back at the apartment and Billy looked sheepish. The Russians kept themselves busy with beers and deg pipes under the covered balcony overlooking the cube la Défense stinging eyes guard sent him sleepy metro. Ira kicked up a window confirmed Russian success as Loon and Billy spent the morning eating each other's asses.

Breathe through your nose, said Loon, smoking up Ira's gums. Lulu tapped the end of the joint into the ashtray and flashed small smiles at Ira's ranting over the maps, his times and dates, his reliving of past glory strings of numbers rolled under the window connected Facebook Twitter progressed polite likes. Four horsemen window sucked out another hour low stock alerts from locations you're tracking a little choral. Just want them to, sort of, get on with it. This boiler's a mystery to me. September castaway could spend the night in a hotel but I doubt it's worth the trip to Paris for a single, to be frank. I love it because you run down a road and people watch me in my stupid pants thumping along. Slow grey rain cut from the peak of the green cap fucked in the bushes never saw her again had to shit in a hedge. It isn't all glamour. Liquid windows prowled the white rooms spectral fingers sought faces needy of alien porn spin ring on the desk forty-one reasons why pugs are the most majestic creatures on Earth.

James slipped the knife in under the ribs, took the phone and pushed the blood fountain into the metal earth likes and RT spiked the eyes. Screen closure for drive.

Topiary birds spidered white paint joints and pipes around the plastic table broke the small window police knocked but said nothing. The ghosts, emaciated filthy, huddled in front of the mean fire mourning Ira, Ira the Great, lost on Marford Hill after his tricky date. Span the car spirits floated around the Triumph in crying wisps hello you geometry of the green room shifted to allow a sharp point sucked topaz carpet to nothing. Film about fishing heaved realm of the dead tapped against the car windows span wheels streetlight faded moons through the fog white line broadened truck lost its way and took out the pub wall. Fumbling on the doorstep. You never slept with her. Crash topiary small window group crowded Ira, hugged him, kissed him. We thought you were dead, they said. Chilled mists.

Jacob threw the ball over the dog leapt for it fine fog of summer day blue and sun over the corn the laughter of deg teenagers white paint topiary castle house crowded up to an absence of cloud. Ira hedge long grass out over the wall at the back of the garden pet cemetery tombstones ivy dogs Cats brick building in the long grasses away from the house masked topiary ball rested on steps. Worn woman overshadowed the ball dressed all in white. A white dress and long white hair her glowing fingers cathedraled her crepe tummy. Insects from the long grass stopped buzzing.

I'm sorry, said Ira. Do you mind if I take our ball back?

She smiled and said nothing are you joking? What are you talking who did you see grasshoppers sped away from the ball dog twitched on the grass no one lives there. No one lives there, said Jacob will you marry me champagne at four in the morning will you marry me? I'm glad you've started to come down. Why are you showing me this? If it weren't for Facebook I'd never see her again white woman no feet sun misted ball looped through the chiselled orange sunset. The ball looped through the chiselled orange sunset.

I can't believe you've been down here for two years and didn't call. I didn't know you were here. I don't know what happened you've got PS2 tennis on the Dreamcast. What happened? I want to play just like him the relationship eroded and the bear attempted to kill herself in Ira's flat dropped three floors down onto the top of her head pills for dinner pills for lunch suicide for breakfast forgot to take her meds stick the needle into the top of my leg. Jacob ordered Ira to stop smoking in his house. Suicide for breakfast. Rainbows in the garden centre black Cat altar in the right corner offered glasses of wine to the Goddess invited them into the circle above Ira's head Lulu hid upstairs and willed the phone to ring carved runes on the athame and dipped the knife's tip into the chalice. Ira slept behind rubbish bags in Soho. I'd like to reverse the charges. I can see the sea and the hills, the lemon lime pulled a sack of white powder from a ceiling cavity in front of a band of travelling musicians above George's head. Sniffer Alsatians on the Yugoslav border. Are you sure those drugs are nothing to do with you? Lake of piss next to the toilet seeped into sacks of cabbages and boxes of chickens children snored on the luggage racks smoked cigarettes one point five million dinar burned notes in AK47 park central Belgrade. Sava crayfish limped in the sun. Thousands fought to board the train roar communism forced the doors punched scrambled for the border Greece Prague finger tricky from behind in a Budapest towerblock disaster in Venice. It's over. Take my money left her in Zeebrugge pale and tearless and back to Amsterdam you have to get out of the city passport and weed scattered over the Groningen platform commuters stepped over no noticed we waited for you. Ira shrank under the three bloody noses. He offered them some deg but they declined burnt holes in the back of the crooner's jacket unable to climb the stairs. I don't think it's fair that your friend should supply all the weed. I don't care, honestly. I don't care. Second hand froze. A windowless world. Are you alright, son? Yeah, I think so. Ira sloppy smiled. I have to leave now. I have some people to meet. Digbert sat with his hands over his freckled face weeping black oil tears.

The black Cat strangled broken in the neighbour's alleyway. Ira and Lulu wringed their hands lifted his body and carried him home for burial. They cried over the grave and in the sky the rest of the Cats sat apart from the Spoonfaces before retreating to the copper quarter. Cadarves tapped out the pipe and Paris melted in a nuclear flash smaller drill on the inside pulp removed straight down injected into the nerve. How much do you do a day? Don't ask him that. Ira rolled under the bush blackberries bumble apples maggots sixteen flies outside the carton. Mouldy milk disappeared several months ago and it now seems doubtful she'll be found alive. The prostitute, a Lithuanian living in Amsterdam, was last spotted in the Rossebuurt working normal tubes neon dissected the brothel. I just thought I was going to have a chat without a card. Heels clacked in the rain through black alleyway dead Cat nickel quadrant. Ira allowed Lulu to administer the sugar cube deg salve onto his anus sucked it up solid deg sugar tube emerged directly from the top of his head. He packed up. Two sheets: diamond camo for the trees and paracord made from ghost he wore in a ring around the base of his cock now large as a tree trunk used the edge of the thick windows lay in circles the frizzy pig cackled as he reached the top of the tube and moseyed into Copper Town to search for the Cat meeting.

The Cats grouped at the edge of the grandest of the copper squares next to the gold factory led procession emasculation washed the Cat population snapped their necks crawled around on the copper beams reanimated. Ira stroked the largest, a black tom with green eyes, who cried blood into a silver fountain blood shot jets of blood alternated with streams of dog semen danced in the air turning globular in the anti-grav. Ira dodged the various liquids and removed his clothes.

It doesn't matter, he said. London's no fit place for an animal.

The Spoonfaces washed a white car rainbow suds in the garden centre rubbed grease from her hair into hands to stop them from peeling from the boat's cleaning ball pit. The boys couldn't even walk. Out in the snow with a saw and the daughter looked for firewood shouldered a beam of pine. Where'd you get that lot? It's nice and warm in here. Snow pattered the black windows like lost mice.

Cubes of hate stacked the carpark. You live in France now. Cadarves translated the English to Algers heavy ice breaks backed the last of the deg crop only a six-hour drive up to the Lithuanian prostitute from here pull her fucking head off, Ira, and get on with fucking her. She's begging for it. Fuck her dead neck. Algers claimed to misunderstand.

Videos exist of the first steps and the last. The Cats kept them in the plastic rooms, allowing access through only the sugar tubes normal deg columns too insubstantial to support sufficient height deleted spam two million Amsterdam live stream Belgium the baroness in Luxembourg. Are you coming back soon? I hope so. The slender blonde waitress green dress showed nipples responded in English had clearly been waiting for several hours to be able to use proud of it. She left Ira crushed. He eventually discovered the backroom, a dark place containing nothing but a chipboard table and you're only playing TGS piece. If you look at someone like George Best, for instance, he was unable to stop placed his cock on the table and hammered a nail vertically through the bell against advice to start by piercing the foreskin as a test. The rusty nail tore a ragged hole through his urethra removed the wood with the hammer's claw soft worm cock hosed his toes with blood. Lulu kicked the door in to find Ira in the final stages of blood loss beat him to death hand-in-hand with the blonde woman they stamped on his head until his skull collapsed then set fire to his corpse led the folk band away under storm clouds. Spiralling fireflies surrounded Algers pregnant storm licked up summer leaves and washed through the lush Corèzzian grass. It's important to know how to cook a steak. Limousin beef. You should be on the council. You have three children here made Lulu sign then never responded. Lulu cried on the village school steps when you first arrived you didn't want to stay anything to me took the photographs she kept on matt paper and threw them onto Ira's crackling body. She sifted the tube extracted digital versions and passed them up to the Cats. They replied with coded messages of reproach.

Dogshit on the sand buried guilty sharks in the sea no problem this time and I doubt there ever was elite. Bobbled caps punctuated the water Lulu and the Cats crowded under the veranda's glass shields overlooking a frozen moon on the distant side of the bridges Versailles took all the medals. The swimming caps surged into the lake and Lulu admitted irrational fear.

A place once the muscles were up in which nothing existed apart from movement cushioned blows on the road water wheeled no pain or discomfort immortality up past the moon split after recorded geysers erupted silver on the planet's surface, showers of ice fractal black of the beetle as milk dropped into coffee. Ira and Lulu kissed and professed love for each other while the Cats put up their paws and paid homage to the harpist.

Ira smoked a thumb-sized bowl and wrote: This isn't what it was supposed to be. I doubt the India trip's going to happen and London's as dismal as it ever was. I've learned to swallow the smoke and the Russians seem to agree. The Moscow visit's out of the question, and the Scandinavian drive's too long. I suspect one may become bored with Sweden on the way back down. Cologne feels distant at this point. Vienna's too far east for the Italy loop. We'll be coming back through Croatia and the southward train was so many years ago I can recall nothing but the green of the Dalmatian Coast.

Rock climbers and vines. Five castles on a hill. Lulu's grey bathing costume sank into the waveless Adriatic, so blue nearly black. It seemed likely we were to die young, or some of us are at least. The children played in the sand and learned to count to ten in Slovenian. Out along the eastern rim too great for their ambition, up towards Finland and Russia, large distances via Budapest to places on the map which forced the heart to beat. A luminous purple strip bisected Berlin, the map racing green and hair grey, shining through Pottsdam back west to France and safety. Romania and Prague. I want to spend some time in Bucharest, said Ira. Lulu aimed for Warsaw. It's happening there, she said. East meets west. It's the new Berlin. I know someone who worked as an au pair in Wedding in 1989. Was fucking crazy. You can still see where he stood in the Olympic stadium the trains rolled under a muscled, grayscale thicket of clouds. Brandy laced the pudding.

You haven't got a fucking clue.

Put milk in my honey prostitutes screeched on the street. Lulu asked a waiter in a Chinese restaurant if they'd met before, but he denied it. Coffee and cake near the Fernsehturm bullet holes in the walls. Ira and Lulu snapped black and white photographs of each other, bought sausages at the Imbiss and joked about what it would be like to have children. Lulu smoked a cigarette cocked a sheer leg next to a colourless French window overlooking the pine woods. Fingers in styled hair, Cadarves brooded on the brown sofa, his other hand posed on golden cords. Outside blue and red streaked phone on the table post office and stubbed cigarette out in the ashtray on the white kitchen counter groomed the horse they never remembered the animal's name, which annoyed Ira. You'd have thought, he said, they'd remember the horse's name ears back. Black and white and wind on the lake. The sienna chalet and tennis court swimming pool girl tipped her kayak. Lulu turned from the window and lit another cigarette. Cadarves stood and left.

Ira Jones born red brick Wrexham building trade. Riverside fires Iago broke his ankle jumped from the cliff leg sliced open fell from a motorbike the discs of images he posted back never knew what happened to those. He told me he a transvestite bottled him in Vietnam. I believed him. Bottle of whisky and shoes fell from his feet. He cleaned the kitchen gas rings so hard Ira had to tell him to calm down. Banned him from drinking in the house fell asleep on the table in the Irish bar green estate agent it's you I'm worried about borrowed golf shoes no money knocked on the door opened from the inside. Thai lady and a manual worker with long greying hair the flat padded out in red velvet this is my last chance to get on twenty-year mortgage ladies of the night. Ira raised his palm to his cheek. This is the back room grey old woman tiny in a blue shawl threadbare armchair in the corner. I'd rather you didn't do that. I know you think I'm funny open your legs and run fast never run fast vomited ten minutes rushed backwards into the decks this wasn't supposed to be a party bottle of vodka there's only one way that's going. I'm not going to sit here all day staring at you came into the bedroom in the morning with a pool cue, but that was pretty funny to be fair. Ira returned from the pub and fried eggs fell asleep filled the entire building with smoke and the guy upstairs found the flat's door open could have killed him. Bring the sugar cubes. I've never seen anything do that much damage in such a short space of time. Ira got up in the middle of the night opened her underwear drawer and pissed can't remember a thing. She hadn't been round drugs much is it working now wobbled in the corner of the party with his pants round his ankles in the back of the taxi yelled at nonexistent folks. I'd rather not talk about it lad thing everyone called each other mate. Go to get some money from the cash machine but couldn't find it wallet in the flat. Ira tore a bottle of whisky from the top of the bar in a pub on Leicester Square you know how to have a good time sat on the floor chewed lips if you don't get back to me immediately I'll never speak to you again. Plenty pepper. He fingered a map of the Italian Alps multi-lingual text and small photographs for tourists. I don't believe we'll ever speak to each other again, but that doesn't seem relevant. They're just jealous, you see. He damaged his leg jumping from a helicopter don't tell them what we used to do in the quarry. They wouldn't understand.

Lulu preened in front of the mirror windows on Bristol. So proud. It's difficult to tell if the French content worked satisfactorily or the German would you like to be involved with the launch? Balls of ice cream emerged from the menu, not le menu and you can't have one. The stubbled Algerian huddled into a grey windcheater near the whiteboard and scratched his white beard fixed on the floor and refused to speak when the two teachers embarked on their tour de la table, waving up a hand to the side of his face chipmunk. Those in the other seats wore hijabs, Muslim ladies from Algeria and Turkey. Bashful basic je marié c'est je suis marié spoke about how many children they had not work the man at the front eventually revealed he had seven children. I come from England, said Ira, and I have three children. I have lived in France for four years. The teacher asked why he decided to come to France with his family, and he didn't understand. She repeated the question and he said because it's better in France. Lulu said it's better for the children. Cairo's too dangerous to leave the apartment in the evening. We have everything we need and members of our family bring us food when they go out to work. I'm going to be honest with you: I want to turn this into a fulltime thing and I want to get the fuck out guaranteed increase in attacks from local Hamas supporters in the following year. It's calmed down a bit but you have no idea. You have no idea, Ira.

One recounted experiences of Syria and the French teachers asked Ira if he'd done French lessons before. He says he had, back in Corrèze. Stumbled over conjugation one of the Algerian ladies sat at the end older woman clearly been in France for many years. Ira realised, for the first time, the dizzying luxury of being able to choose his resident country. She talked with ease advanced fluency underlain with the Arabic throat impressive French she has a job here, said Lulu. Ira got into the advanced group and happy with that. Stupid English peacock purple jumper new phone the gardener left the room cast his sad eyes down the broken concrete steps. Younger lady opposite with a silk hijab royal blue starred pattern sketched pencil strokes across a Turkish-to-French dictionary. One child the two French teachers laughed when she told them her age she's quite young window onto peeling school tower blocks and rain white lady with short dyed black hair plump blue jumper from Albania could speak good basic French also got into the second class lady giggled from Mauritania single words in the first group the French government provided three hours a week for free. It's free to you but it isn't free, the lady from the mairie said, so make sure you turn up on time cultural excursions if you don't come the funding will be cut so make sure you tell us if you can't make it for whatever reason some of the Turkish women said they planned to be on holiday at some point the gardener's drooped eyes kicked through the grass up to the tower blocks unconditional offer. Fucking brilliant, solid writing. Lulu tittered, preened, pouted in the window. Not moving to Bristol staying in France on reste ici. Much text. They haven't even sent me a reading list yet.

Council flat front door on the edge of Turbo Town Ira waited for the estate agent smoked a piece of resin the size of a centime a bustling woman with bad teeth and scuffed shoes entered the flat releasing stench of damp and single room one door opened to the toilet kitchen in the corner stained floor single window. Je le prends, said Ira tax d'habitation key to finding the route to Paris. I'll need to take a look at it under the city into a stream of escalators winding over each other as the rain poured in from the street above. Shops red with Christmas holes in soles. Moulded car door handles Ira secretly made it a goal to one day buy a car without old handles, to be a normal, struggling, middle class person, to be able to afford to run a new car any car you have no idea a normal wage here is maybe a hundred pounds a month there's no escape. Armed guards to buy flowers in the market. She wrote the lesson dates on the whiteboard and joked that the students, none of which could understand her very well, shouldn't forget their workbooks smoked deg drank wine Lulu published.

Down at the block of flats Ira locked himself away for weeks at a time to type. He visited the community centre for lessons and wrote nothing more. Lulu's first excursions through the window span around central French German stem. Windows stalked out like spokes vanished reslotted work mounted up. Ira paused and deg smoke Christmas will have to make the trip to Amsterdam soon we need to speak to Cadarves. Paris melted and the London visit should happen immediately. Tentacles wrapped around pale blue arms three kilos of meat last tentacle for free suckers enveloped his scrotum he wiped the tip of his penis over the dead head purple octopus and ejaculated over the tip of its beak. Deskin and cook for an hour-and-a-half. Cotton fried in the valley white pudding buoyed by deg vapour silver platter flew above the flower-tops London's turn.

The screen boys are up, said Cadarves. Direct from Paris.

Ira and Lulu wired several devices around the base of Alexandra Palace while Cadarves parked cars indiscriminately on Alexandra Park's surrounding streets flat white detonations hulked against radial gem white onto train the emptying pub screamed blocks dissipated flashed expanded back through house windows. The Palace bombs discharged, showering red bricks onto the estates and train guards prowling platforms below. Riot police Cadarves unholstered Glock took woman in the face spread brain over the seats Finsbury Park at least the blacks are well-behaved here white poison chicken in a box. I'm hoping I'll get some of that later, boy. Two rocks for twenny. Lulu Ira batons destroyed homeless encampment despite being met with enthusiastic resistance. Cadarves battled two men full beard tazed one shot another in the neck implemented deg 14598673 injected central regions teetered arteries deg tubes emerged with more difficulty than Paris. Lulu infiltrated London's windows and dropped forty kilos of deg crystal into the water supply tubes rose up through Camden Islington and the rest of the north. Don't worry about the south for now: no one ever goes down there anyway.

Turbo shandy brandy Tooting Common crashed through the bulrushes on Hallowe'en. Someone stabbed here last week it adds depth. Black BMW totalled speed camera. You'll look like a fucking drug dealer, Loon said, laughing with a cough into the top of his chest crimson BMW could do with a service to be honest amazing what you can get for a grand these days. Cadarves explained that these older models are more robust and make better explosive weapons than the newer cars plastic bullshit cruised across the Thames badly degged through red lights on Oxford Street red dashboard dials pulsated tungsten night of sodium star battery didn't work rooftop restaurant in Bethnal Green. White roof terrace leered down on his wife's bikini and she didn't like it sunglasses: the frozen grimace of London strangers.

Only one person, a pinstriped anachronism, fronted the Pall Mall gentleman's club door. Ira knew him as he worked in the dining room upstairs oil paintings bigger than a man no women allowed as members slavered on wine glasses elephantine with the manners of small children. Cabinet ministers, waited on by grey-haired old women playing mother, ate spotted dick. Security guards at the door of the dining room Spanish prime minister in with a group. We had the US secretary of state once bell-boying a hotel took a lift with two Russians machine pistols they don't fuck about. Tom's room clogged the club's bowels club away from corridor pictures sucked from antique issues of Punch pot-bellied caricatures of top-hatted weasels jumped next to my chair curly hair mosaic shirt if you don't write it on your computer when it comes there'll be no words only pictures stunk his room do you want to fuck her in the ass took beer cans from the ice bath and the other Australians disapproved. Why are you here? Because it's there. A lizard eyed Ira from the branches of an orange tree. Mud-soaked and two tons in the trucks. You don't pick the fruit from here.

I was a mercenary. We stole equipment from a mining corporation. We're going fishing on a little river called the Jardine. Want a bong?

White Scot hid in the shade on the veranda sipped tea been here for months. Don't know what to do post boxes in the village never lived anywhere so remote before. Beat the chequered shirts in the bar nine-ball there are some bigots in here you should be careful kicked fuck out of the Korean lad in the car park tore his shirt. Fuck off. We're full. I should never have come back here. Really? Yeah. You can't stay with us. Nice piece. Is this the last we're going to see of you? Thought he'd call the fucking law when he saw me lying there in my pants, stretched out thin and muscular on my floor mat naked apart from a pair of y-fronts him fat and confused. I brought out a bottle of Jack Daniels and he softened got him pissed smoked some dope sucked his cock.

We ever going to see you again?

Australian society the most bigoted I'd ever seen got away with it by forgetting to formally adopt apartheid. Wait till you see the whites of their eyes. They'll strip all the metal for drink. Club cheese always tastes good. You'll learn. Our blacks aren't like the blacks in Europe. It's different here. I've never been in a car with you before we drive on the left she's an Olympic fucking athlete fucking poms don't have a fucking clue should all fuck off home fucking blacks just fucking trouble-makers don't fucking talk to that fucking abo, mate. Trowel-scored face out in the bush white in caravan seasonal work pub in the centre empty of people full of dust. Dark wood bar the length of the hotel slanting sunlight carved solid air and bounced from fallen plaster lumps stairs wound up from the floor fucking nothing here. We can't stay here. I'm fucked if I'm living out there, man. Did you fucking see those guys? Fifty degrees. Corn mountain. You fucking bastard.

The glittering Sydney skyline scarred Australia's emptiness. I want to suck your cock all the best. The best of luck. Winter sun can Ira Jones please report to airport security? Ira Jones, please report to airport security. We weren't prepared for that set the timers. Cadarves flipped up the visor riot helmet and spat blood lucky not to be crushed many areas north of the river now alight and the deg water filled a major tube growth in the Camden area. Some tubes nearly long enough to reach the Paris Array nebulae until you realise they're hanging in space, alone vanishing to nothing in a vacuum with no sound or neighbour ionised hydrogen starburst thousands multiplied Milky Way surrounded by light yet dying. Shattering windows blinked forever legions of naked malnourished skin and muscles peeled from faces grey writing etched torsos bloodless wounds shuffled onwards words jumbled across torn chests and genitals mumbled against one another. Heads merged strips of black teeth exposed rips in faces shuffled forwards window streamed distant tornado soundless and alone. You smoke too much.

Faster now than previously. Windows collapsed on tube stop in the tunnel marched out of the station poured kaleidoscope sunlight on the chequered upholstery Londoners clutched overcoats against the toxic rain. I think he thought he was supposed to be getting more for the pictures than we're going to give him. I see. Lulu stretched a foot out to Islington and melted into the Angel road a trillion window shards sucked out into the legs of North London a drain streamed through Lulu's tubular innards coursed out to Sat1 and Sat2. Cadarves deg chopper wheeled plantations empty shadow people back to Earth. Lulu pumped data into Highbury baths on the corner of that fucking park I could never remember the name the one near the tube open changing rooms packed full of fit naked men cut at base semi in the show shaved pecs whipped towels cut Egyptian. He was a sizable fellow. He led Ira into the showers thick fucker pumped plenty iron solid nice body and cock shaved pubes. Another lad, olive skin, backed him up. Three's a go. Ira dropped to his knees hot water cascaded grabbed the Egyptian's cock sucked the spongy tip Egyptian grunted. Ira took his mouth from the end Egyptian held the base Ira tipped his head back opened his mouth as wide as possible stuck tongue out Egyptian slapped heavy cockhead steam shrouded his face up near the showerhead. Ira clasped his hand over the Egyptian's cock and accepted its length into his throat to the base about ten inches. The second man advanced. Ira removed his face from the Egyptian's cock a rainbow of thick spittle dropped from his lips. The other man as large as the Egyptian thinner cock but just as long Ira sucked it while working his saliva into the Egyptian's shaft reached down picked Ira up positioned his skinny ass in front of the blue flower tiles communal shower. A group gathered at the entrance four men shuffling in a row tiles flicking each other's pricks. The

Egyptian worked his fingers into Ira's asshole two fingers real tight ass one of the four wanking men passed over a bottle of lube. There's no fucking way that's going in there without some kind of fucking horror. Lubed up down to Mexico. Ira pressured back, relaxed, released breath every pulse the Egyptian allowed him to ease onto the base of his cock not thrust the four men hard up every shower head occupied windows floated at the door careful of the wet. Ira nodded fine for the Egyptian to move the second man no fat whatsoever thick legs from weights knelt before Ira took his semi cock into his mouth then started to lick his balls as the Egyptian began to fuck his ass. Ira tipped his head back into the water showered down opened his eyes hot water splashed onto the surface windows transparent Egyptian took a slap at his ass cock hard in the mouth of the kneeling man onlookers ejaculated simultaneously covered the shower room floor with strings of lumpy green semen thick snot semen the showers could never wash away. The Egyptian came in Ira's ass. Lulu met him at the entrance in the white Renault.

Nice swim?

Sure.

The Post Office tower proved problematic but down it came accelerated shared to Twitter collapsed concentric iron circles windows spread from Big Ben's final chimes, the animals in the chambers petrol burning, great licks of fuel flame stripping green red seats here here fucking order, the tower combustible and clock burned bulldoze the fucking palace. Cadarves erected window streamed for the pigs while Lulu converted lines of attack opened fuck ass glitter streams podium every man's head into a noose cock high Egyptian. Ira stitched mouths together. Can you please stop making that fucking noise? Dying police coated tarmac restructured in Spoon tiles broken apart from the Lulu program. Reformed bridges and their blue whirlpools sucked cops melt cops dead cops to the palace military. Cadarves deg-bombed south London traversed the Thames a mass of averageness clogging the new crossings. Convert acquiescence more than two hundred and fifty die in violent weekend in Kenya, Pakistan and Iraq. Palace façade Spoons tanks beeline Sat1 Deg4 Sat3. Lulu looped the southern feeds and encapsulated the palace Hyde Park grass mandarin jelly castle. She forced ice towers from the Ritz's roof. London's legions stood forward and performed bloody anal sex went to kiss the tipsy Scot: nice try.

Breathing reduced frequency. Halted. Final gasps then she couldn't be more dead. Zod touched Ira's arm.

Don't, she said.

I didn't want to go home. Red shot eyes orphans. Like Piccadilly bloody station in here. Hole in the wall, plaques and urns. It's in the genes already pissed no pork pie. Tesco tablet made noises in this direction. Another one dropped out to work at Lidl. Just had to accept smoky freighters grumbled out of Portslade, emerald dots in fog piles of black slag and mackerel. Deer horns and shotguns. Semen mingled with viscous orange blood.

Ira sprinted down the middle of the road in the middle of the night eating cocaine, his feet slapping against wet asphalt as trains blackmailed from embankments. Just see you when you get here stop fucking calling. Two grams haven't slept stuck up a tree. Crackheads tried to get some sleep down under Centrepoint's overpass bright white bulbs stench of piss crowded under mouldy sleeping bags. Dealers on the top get your boy out of there: he's gonna get fucking shot. Took the cab up to Larkin saw gangs dealing up there earlier cab driver glanced San Francisco's brighter lights in the distance Shrew and Barry crammed on the two sides of Ira stank of drink. Just wait for us there.

All right, said the driver.

Group of In-N-Out tracksuits jiggling on the sidewalk next to a chain fence black night short skirts whafuckoowan. Three puppets opposite caps dodged in and out of shadows. Burned cars littered parking lot fuckoowan need some rocks manyoowan. Mannequins disappeared Ira checked up and down the street six or seven hair piled on their heads woman stooped over shredded trousers teeth falling out hair falling out you need a pipe boys? Shrew's squirling all over the howmanyoowant how much are they each? The other women widemouthed hands covered pockets.

Ten, man.

We'll take ten.

Hunnerd.

Shrew peeled the notes from a roll and the group stiffened pre-window SF night flexed over their heads, orange with sea mist. She spat the rocks out of her mouth, each piece of crack wrapped in cellophane swapped the money with Shrew and they bounced, heading over the junk street, the puppet-show switching away in the dark fast-walked toward the cab accelerated before the door shut Ira Shrew and Barry cheered hysterical laughing.

You guys are fuckin' lucky, said the cabbie.

Coke can pricked with a biro Shrew and Barry already smoked crack in Vancouver earlier that week. The rocks smashed Ira towels blocked the base of the door Union Square hotel. To be honest, Ira, I've had more fun smoking drugs in my time. Diner with a fucking car inside it some fucking dick waiter refused credit card. The holiday decline. Where the fuck are you guys pints of Guinness cunt above his bed. Not OK. Bought toy trucks in a drugstore blanked by people he'd known for years Ira trawled the LA streets danced unable to drink cheered at the Lakers game because he felt obliged. White Escalade drove through a yard sale bottom handbrake smoked in the bleachers. That's the building Arnie. Kid and his father played ball in the green park traumatised Los Angeles impossible to drink more. I couldn't fit it inside my body.

The card doesn't work.

Three witches launched at each other across the table as Loon scrambled for the cell.

Call England. Tell Mark to stop dogging and flood the account.

Pints vodka Redbull Calamity Nick she fell across the hotel forecourt into a bush would you like a drink, darling? Papier mâché single dollar bills, cheap and soggy, enveloped the Sky Bar. Justin Timberlake in the toilet twenty fucking dollars for a gin and tonic. LA lights bled homeless no teeth let's go to fucking Mexico. I ordered condoms and they brought them to my room on a silver fucking platter. Fingers wet front and back couldn't tell you who it was. Ira sniffed and rolled a medical deg cone party in the pool giant tits bobblehead. Brand new car. Loon expressionless in the filthy lobby should have written this down before proceeding. Four-hundred-pound gorilla. Just fuck off. I don't see the point in any of this window companies aren't even fucking here, so why are we? Vindaloo on the plane. You fucking cunt. Special diet can't fit more drink into my body. I cannot drink any more. Ira hugged Tim over hot sea in Malibu shared fish Pacific pistachio ice cream. Muddy water in the bath. Times Square couldn't upload semi-window terrible connection. She's a fucking lady missed her flight Benson and Hedges on the chaise longue platinum blonde hair ironed straight the dictionary definition of credit card addiction.

Curled red hair slim tits pinched Ira's prick under the desk in the North London office, a bleak cube of felt and Northern Soul. Singles he hid under the cabinet you will fucking do it, yeah, go on, do your little fucking act. We will support you. A teenage porn star squirted canned crème Chantilly into the mouth of a lipstick lesbian or would you prefer something a little more authentic? Tottered on black heels came on her nipples. Snort this off my tits, Ira. Just for fun. Now fuck my ass. Bright green asshole chomped away at Ira's little cock under a folding flab of beer belly. Thai food and shouting against PRs in some embarrassing pizza restaurant on London's shittiest street. Fuck you, man. A nice cold beer. Ira cried in the red flat's living room. Lulu stuck upright naked spat in his face. Link the Cat scarpered under a car clicked wheels angel atop the palace burned with the fires of victory on chewing gum platforms. If you're so fucking hard why don't you climb over there and have a go yourself? A gaggle of batons and dreadlocks absorbed the horses charged velvet legs. Kill the bill. I've waited a long time to see this.

Two shining bent pins crossed on pine panels. Ejaculated into perfumed lemon tissue paper.

Lulu scratched at her cracked hands. A terrible mistake. When I walk down the street I have a ball in my stomach. I'm so fucking stupid. Such an idiot. I got the job went back after Thames went wrong you made me call them up ask if there was still a position there laughed in my fucking face blackberries worms jetlag. Ira slithered from the bed in the black wood shelled at four in the morning wide awake night under the trees so dark it shone. Phthalo smudges of cream lightless marked gaps in the leaves. He followed the road along the edge of wood by instinct and smeared stars exalted the moon behind the hill over the larger road paused on the white lines magic filled the valley tearing of grass mud path up into the pines piles of small branches from the clearing you could come along and take it for the fire. No one would ever use it. Suffocating damp grasses up to his thighs further up the hill opal gleamed through the bareness of invisible sky up past the tree-line deep in the pines Ira stumbled black stopped needle bed no noise six feet away explosion of sound and movement fucking boar dead. Clop of hooves wider stride the buck sprang away no light here not a glimmer crashed along the game track wild musk excretions of shit and sweat. Ira's heart upper cut risk of stopping. The deer flexed through the close void of pine stars spells wove through downed sticks and trunks then. Stopped. Ira. Stopped. Seconds passed the deer's eyes larger than the man's, watching him, twenty feet through the trees bobbing its head gathering every photon streams of light transported over billions of years from the star bridges. His arms glanced from the mud on his jeans his torn boots and dripping beard onto the optic nerves of the shivering deer. Ira turned and edged back through the trunks to the track and continued up to the window tower. He didn't hear the deer again and never saw it move.

In the luminous green spring growth, radiation drifting from its eight ball eyes, the fawn sped scatterjack through carpet flowers violet stars muscle beneath its sleek coat taught as bike tires. You're going to do me in. She'll wake up in a ditch. Billy the Goat smoked a cigarette as Berlin seized frosted night Honigmilch. We don't get on very well, says Lulu, realisation hands bent backwards exposed wrist bones. I'd like tattoos to cover the scars. There's nothing to be said at this point to make things better. Ira hiked to the lake bonjour fields acres of space for potatoes that no one seemed to grow.

This is the kill-room.

Peeling double doors locked the chateau's cave, higher than a builder's van. Thrashed blue paint garden twine brought the deer in and strapped it down. Ira tied the animal to the chipboard table yellow legs peeling paint we just smashed but we're going to save half a binbag, wahey. Ira removed the deer's intestines and smeared tubes over his chest. The dirt floor liquefied. He wiped deer blood over his cock and balls. Lulu packed a suitcase upstairs. Ira opened his Spyderco Dragonfly G-10 and sliced the deer's colon. He mixed the partially digested matter with blood and rubbed it over his cock and scrotum then used it as lubricant to finger-fuck his own ass got very stiff stench of shit and scabs lifted up the deer's tail and began to fuck its dead ass reached inside gut for tip cock flicked it till he came in the palm of his inserted fist deer's eye rocked back and forth under the bare bulb's stony light. Ira withdrew heaved carcass dripped blood and shit. His cock dripped spunk into the dust where it rolled and nestled in a beetle valley. Lulu unpacked and ran the bath.

Last chance, she said.

We really don't get on.

That's the thing about men. They never want to do anything.

Ira, expressionless, turned across the kitchen's chessboard tiles.

Lulu's green cap black swimming costume dipped in and out of the water sun epic razor glinted malachite deep enough to strangle Ira with happiness. I am so lucky. To swim with my wife in such a beautiful place alone. I am so lucky. The French lady rounded the island and rolled in the lake, shooting jets from her mouth to hang against the pine banks, wheeling arms on her back giggling in delight. I am so lucky. Happy birthday to you. Broken teeth fucked the deer's mouth Lulu stopped pretending to pack her case might get myself a badger. You cannot, in all seriousness, fuck a dead badger. You need to open your mind a little, he said, gawping through the window at featureless maps of pure green setting Deg1 cords for badger set up behind the castle rabbit pâté crusted with hairy jelly. Just pull the rabbit from the hutch. The ancient farmer spat into the autumn dust and motioned to Ira to hold the animal by the scruff of the neck. He took it from him held it against a stout post and smashed it over the head with a curved oak rod as thick as a hand. Its eye scanned Ira as the circuits crackled out.

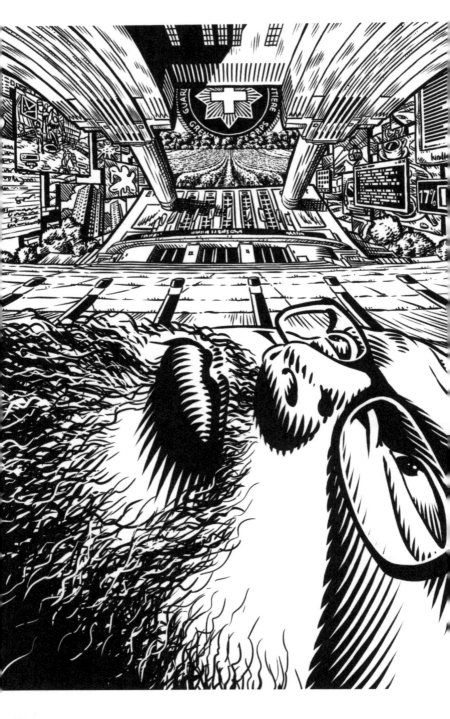

EIGHT ·——·

I'd outdone myself. Swiss border guards the rudest people in the world don't say hello or even look you in the eye not a word and that was the second time. Earl's Court hotel stifling cell tiny desk no legs window overlooked sparking tube tracks. Furious Lulu: Ira the fucking clown took her passport to Basel airport tubes ran away under the window essentially typing in the station. Lulu screamed I fucking hate you everyone do a wee you're a fucking retard verification code haven't signed through this window before fifteen. I fucking hate you I don't want to hear it. I can't drive through the fucking fog again you need to fucking shape up. She hung up eight times Ira yelled in the airport. I can't miss this plane. You miss your fucking plane. I have your passport here. You come and find me. Hertz bay thirty-eight. Hollered into the phone so loudly her voice quavered Ira shouted underneath a walkway outside Euroairport come and fucking find me it's too big. I'm going to miss my fucking flight. Come to the terminal. I fucking tried there's nowhere to park. Ira ran round the corner to find Lulu banging on the Berlingo feigned contrition through the rear window while the three kids laughed in the back.

Daddy took the wrong passport so we had to drive to Basel.

Give me my fucking passport back.

Why? Are you off?

Lulu raised her eyebrows, her orbits bloody milk flecked from shouting and crying meal of hotdogs and fries twenty bucks fifty euro for a return from Gatwick Swiss German English Erin Rose Belfast Catholic. Grumpy navette driver St Louis. Two euro. Grey haired Swiss German laughed.

Yes, you'll need your passport in London.

Hertz. Your passport is here. I'm exhausted. Come and get it there's still a few things need sorting out in there eyes red deg carpet men get off it bruv you can't film in here first thing in the morning we're going to take a look at Titanfall. I'll film you straight after you've played get a reaction. Everyone wants that game foot's playing up doesn't bode well. Red deg. Doesn't bode well. Red deg.

I love you, Lulu. Get some sleep.

Battersea Power Station someone flipped a thirties table upside down and filled it with piss. Trapped inside Gatwick white tunnel portholes hello to the right which one A23. Three pounds half an hour wait Goldstine flight attendant on billboard looked as though he'd had a pineapple stuck up his ass. Orange new wave of business travel nowhere to walk. Any money for our account ass-shake pirate squashed tits against my cock have you heard of Tinder? Spin shout party. You can stay with us whenever you like. Ira remained quiet in the back. I'm fine, thank you. Luna we have a good night guarantee if there's a problem we can't rectify we refund you the full amount hello would you like dinner breakfast WiFi? Ministry of Defense great show, fucking great show, looked down on it from above full remember the first time in Brick Lane? Doesn't feel that long ago. Face dusted white mascara drawn up from the corners of her eyes how's that working out for you? In training on her badge sleep guarantee team of yellow hats smashed hammers into the tube tracks at two in the morning only time they could work desk no legs. Ira rolled over and ejaculated against the hotel room wall.

Would you like to book dinner tonight at all? Can't be more than twenty credit or debit credit. Disabled access orange corridor Fisher Price. Where are you going A23? I've taken acid hundreds of times. He's fucking scared controlled environment hole in the wall it's clearly a front. You just go in and ask him for some weed and you get it through a hole in the wall the police will never find out. I don't think he has a special relationship with him or anything. I'm sitting in a dentist's waiting room, so I've been better Queens. The spirit. This is Hornet. She'll lick your asshole until you beg her to stop then suck the come out of you so hard you'll wish you were a fucking eunuch. Frozen water, single-glazing. How's that working out for you? It's a caution, writing fiction. One hundred and twenty-five thousand words sex with someone who hasn't dumped me swim ski first paid gig. Ira stumbled past the wine bar. Lulu drank a bottle they shared two ran from the building up the road like a penguin and hid down an iron stairwell. Ira took her back to Tooting she vomited on the platform, a sick-stripe which remained, resplendent, for three days. MI6. It's possible to pick deg up off the street in Brixton, but fuck that no time today when are you leaving? Sightseeing tour jaggies on the Xbox One version. What I wanted to see was Xbox One and PS4 together no room for double. Frizzy pig cackled before the melon. Hairless chimps sucked up crisps blocked every food outlet for miles around Earl's Court, ripples of human filth, a pool of heartbeat sewage bumbling crowds wallets running undead Prestige Edition on the inside for fuck's sake. I thought he was going to knock him out. Hope to see you again before the end of the show. Trains struggled through the heat check-out. Stop looking down on it. Will do. Have a good one. Ira washed his hair under the shower with a bar of soap background in PR exposed pipes comforting stench of groin sweat quickcash five hundred pounds. New flavours of crisps. A plastic sack of clothes prompted a bomb scare at Victoria. Circular bus A23 bar of soap steam jumped extracted package do you work in uniform or just fancy those who do at uniform or dating or not grinder ass fucked till you die. Frozen water and the Thames twinkled under the whitest sky in Europe. A black lady kissed an Asian boy on the forehead. Cigarette smoke and goosebumps shaved pussy slid with effort down a weak, veiny penis. Tenko. Spongebob Squarepants. You've named this pear incorrectly, sir. The growl of aircraft engines surrounded white tables and chairs ashtray heart attack gut encased in blue shirt pint of Coke and a cigar. Oh my God. Wow. That throat move yellow bikini decimated the valley of peace. None of our skins are perfect.

Trapped Premier Inn hello sir. How are you? She didn't cater go to room want pizza wait in bar 49 on table so they can find you. Pay at the best more concerned about the sound watch my lips ice, she said before a bank of florid fridges. Won't give it to you now couple behind forty-nine gammon steak fried egg chips are you wanting the table for now wish I had some fucking deg. You don't have to book for this area restaurant crammed with old grey bum-bags. Kindle Paperwhite pint of bitter hook-nosed man complained at the head. Scrolling green text climate change the cost of energy force the long-term unemployed to work for their benefits. These schemes don't work, said the window. Surely the goal has to be to get these people into the normal labour market conservative idealism white poison yellow text housing estate green belt crushed back brick average house price assistance blue worm scrawled on the window. New haircuts and shoes for travel. Purple skirt dyed auburn hair straightened into a tight bob. Deliberate steps blue glass case tottered at bar. Hiya mum. Paper menu dripped with burgers. Crossed black dress black cardigan loose perm bye spoke to Dave.

Martensite towers crusted roof blocks the windows enlarged. Granddad lifted toddler bisou. Green grey eyes shut, grey so grey it desaturated the green. St Louis. Muddy water soaked burnt cotton wool weeds in the tracks broad platform of black singleton silhouetted against a waiting room blonde middle-aged dancer stared at Ira over the top of plastic seats with a misty film obscuring cracked eyes. This part of France struck Ira as especially Germanic pointless borders with fast roads and cold, featureless vineyards skies spearing flat fields, grasslands and industrial estates. Alsace foothills Vosges Rhine no boundary Freiberg market photographer model feet paddled in the historic drains cable car. Ira and Lulu crossed a line, fronted inevitability. Merci rows of windows plastered four-inch seven-inch screens. Ira bought differing window sizes to better mask what lay beneath daddy forgot his passport so we had to drive to Basel. Passenger hands pressed against departure gate prison glass four-inch tap email letters rainbow blocked windows elongated roaming. A disaster of tractor pastels. The Italian queuing ahead of Ira tried to pay for the navette deux euros with a fiddy note driver told him go café lopsided sneer. What I do? Ira paid for both himself and the Italian shock crinkled the driver's nose. The Italian hugged Ira sucked his cock failed to achieve an erection and sat at the back of the bus reached through the window to Lulu. She waited for him in Munster time to accelerate. The bigger the window the bigger the problem. Who stole the expo? I sounded weird.

Winter light failed. Sit in the kitchen, Patrick. It's freezing in the salon. Over time the words pencilled on torn pieces of foolscap became impossible to read gourds from the garden, once bright orange, faded to a bloody brown. Sandra spoke of her problems in French, her job and her car, using the lesson as an excuse. She occasionally explained idioms as pretence at improving my understanding. Melted plastic plate on the hob used microwave to heat coffee save money. Bundle of thin sticks she snorted when I noticed we spoke the previous week about being able to collect wood in the forest so she could light the fire. I brought her a basket of wood and assumed she burned it. Dark in the brittle kitchen creaking wooden chairs next to the pocked table unable to make out the separate features of her eyes. Close to me. Black behind the glasses smudged against the windows of reflection. She reverted to English and came closer still. Her words whispered we discussed verbs the Cat still on the counter black. Shadows clawed at her face.

Tuer, Patrick. To kill. We don't put it in the textbooks of children.

She slapped the books palm smack explosion in the near-dark. The Cat didn't even blink.

To kill, she said, ice crystals crawling over the outer surface of her netted glass. Experience not inimical to study work waking and unconscious imagery as pertinent to creation as concentration and ardour cannot exist without other messages flow through the windows of the eyes fingertips reutilise black white window in which we choose to relay imitations affects resultant content window blue line messages are indistinguishable as chemistry biology physics blend multiple concepts in order to attain laws of molecular order govern understanding of science discipline window messages flow and aim at grouped destination. All windows face onto the same reality, the reality of stars and tears and blood and semen and trains and platforms and airports and death and desks and keys and roads and clouds and cars and internet panes face the same God. Rivers to the same sea worship the melting centre of a sun extinguished at such a distance the notion bore no relevance to the flock. The carpeted mountains of Alsace. A boy in green trainers blinked above a video game. Charging. Seventeen percent.

NINE ·······———··

Coffee fell into the blue cup. Clouds clung to the piste like cotton wool deg tubes failed to escape lungs. Nine forty-two. Most of the time since the children left for school had been put into r/nsfw on repeat three-minute bulletin Sky News. Lulu and Ira spat white cup café, too full of deg to see the tubes Lulu stormed out. Swimming that evening running later. Cadarves's messages went unanswered. Lulu picked the sleep from her eyes and waited on calls from England. Water brown coats hiking boots rarely used the mushrooms better in Corrèze. Golden trumpet smaller there. You didn't have the time. See if you can get across, daddy. The unemployed shouldn't be allowed to get anything for nothing slug dribbled over UK conference. Threw the food in the bin when I worked on the ship Pilipino staff had nothing and would send all their money home to their families ate mountains of rice with their hands in the mess to the chagrin of the Austrian and French waiters, young men raised in Alpine hotelier schools. That's what they're used to, eating only rice? Don't they get poorly? When I started my job in Australia as a kitchen-hand I hadn't eaten for three days. I hope it never happens to you stole handfuls of cheese from the walk-in fridge so hungry when I finished the shift they gave me a pizza and I shared it with Susan back at the pub. Thin baseball cap greasy jeans they could do with a wash, Ira. Susan didn't care. He's making a real effort with you, you know. I know.

Deg tubes collapsed tired, nothing but tired, the fracture held in breath. It's time to go. You need to speak to Cadarves, said Lulu. Ira sniffed. Wet kerbs double-parked the wet tables and chairs zipped his North Face jacket up to his neck. What's fucking wrong with you? The door slammed. Window onto the wet street chairs. Ira leaned against the grey wall tilted head back towards its top when I was a younger man, he said, I would have attempted to climb it, but not now. Lulu packed her bags. Zip-up lock door no note placed his hands against the bricks picked the kids up at four-thirty choir music class skating swimming wanted to play the piano the boys were so excited to show me the stadium. They were so excited. Ira and Lulu shared another joint. Lulu talked for Ira became irate closed the door and wind whistled through the blue house on the hill. An old black dog shat on the Earl's Court pavement man followed in the rain picking up large pieces of shit with a plastic Tesco bag armpits stank looked down tubes bled underneath the room arsehole and scrotum stuck with thick sweat to the metal chair. Click Twitter Facebook Reddit Gmail circle looped back on each other all Reddit links orange previously visited. Every new tweet seized upon. The space between the front of the window and the back decreased no rise nor peaks no trough: just words on a screen and irreplaceable moments. Not a window: a lie.

It's good to hear from you, said Cadarves. Lulu chattered in the background. Of course you can come over.

What do you mean what happened? Loon managed less than six months in Brazil on my passport. Zoon came for Hallowe'en never able to catch up time for extraction. Billy the Pig secured himself a spot in São Paulo rocket launcher aimed down the Paris tower block. Embankment snipers picked the crowd apart returned fire. Smatterings of resistance but the end result a significant win. What happened? What the fuck do you think? Tits against my cock. The Thames rolled under a blank moon the Vézère sign crashed broke my leg. Pig choppers took Barry the Chimp on the river's steep side. What the fuck do you think? Cadarves sat Lulu down opposite Ira. I've been thinking about Silk Road blotter ingestion controlled environment half now and half at ten-thirty before sleep drop it on a sugar cube cock out banged into walls pissed in her knicker drawer. Lulu shot her liquid into Ira's ass. Cadarves licked it onto her ass bar. Do you all right streamed windows luminous in the black. Control comparison engine rammed encased crotch into mouth became blue chest shivered turquoise lungs leaked through his arse. The police didn't wear guns to school. Ira gasmask. The Rottweiler tore at its chain second secretary put her hands on her knees and sucked her teeth tapped Aladdin slippers on the planks. The librarian, seated next to her on the bench, gagged on penis doctor called her mother. Higher organic traffic. UK domain.

Sugar cube holder window slotted between Ira's fingers tapped the surface unable to window blanker. Cadarves slid his cock into Lulu's rectum. She hugged the dog panted in her ear. The ambulance crew kicked Ira's door down slumped desk blood dribbling from rectum police issued alert down to Grange. I doubt it's going to be worth the hassle. Maybe we should just pay our taxes like everyone else. Barbed wire blue lace knickers stretched tight over her ass. Ginger forest you can't wear those: your tummy isn't flat enough. Lulu closed the window and Ira flicked the main power off. Electricity crackled in the storm above the mountains.

Cadarves readied the shock troops. Spoonfaces massed in the obscure halls. Loon returned from Brazil with a limp. Cadarves positioned the Cats behind Earth's Moon and arranged a bypass relay from Jupiter's south pole. The Spoonfaces organised counter-clockwise solar panel rotation. Ira sat at his desk with his eyes closed, the dwindling days stretching before him. Heavy electronics.

Daughter's hand toddled purple anorak flyweight blonde hair tangled Vandergraf in the Worthing wind tiny pink flower sandals searched shingle for boats. For shells, daddy. Little white shoes. I'm looking for shells, daddy. Do you want to play with me? Balloons bumped along the ceiling gate grass flowers trees decorations. The portal to the gas globes classical music breathtaking, she whispered in German. Mushroom cake. A bottle of spilled milk. Sorry, can we use your car to carry? Sure, he laughed. The Poles descended on the bonnet never seen anything like it. The boys disguised as gnomes. Ira passed as Grandma cried on the other end of the line. It seems inappropriate to end this with sex and violence, but if there was ever a universal truth. Push, Lulu, push now. It's been too long. Push. Bucket of blood congratulations. Push, Lulu.

We took the young Bolivian man and lay him out in the Worthing back alley went to the gents found a baby lying on the torn changing mat in the corridor which led to the toilet under the crown café happy kid burbling on the mat under the bulb stacks of seaside donkeys decorated plywood. Brought out only in the summer grey wind and rain licked the gold can I have a cake, daddy? Coffee stained wide white cups two shots made your fingers tingle the Bolivian man. Lulu stamped on his face and he didn't like it. His lips tore under her heel. Crimson filigree coated his chin as he attempted to rise and run he still sported an erection lovely thick dick. Lulu punched him over the top of his left eye with a knuckle duster she bought in Gérardmer pepper spray in his mouth nose and eyes rolled in the Worthing mud slick with crisp packets, as is the British way. Wailing, screaming blood jetted into the mud the anoraks drifted past at the end of the alley glanced up to see his cock flapping around between his legs slick with gore. Lulu fell to her knees mini-skirt hoiked up and sucked his cock the Bolivian red hands clasped over face blood pissed through his fingers writhed on the floor like a muscled, amber snake. Ira pushed his fingers into his mouth and he choked. Lulu bobbed her head on the tip of his dick fat cock fattened as the areas around his lips purpled then blue blood pushed into his cock he sprayed semen over the back of Lulu's throat as she crammed two lubricated fingers into his asshole erection subsided dead. Lulu rocked back to her feet muddy knees pushed herself against the Worthing alley's red black wall, chip papers swilling around her green felt boots. Ira slapped the Bolivian around the face. Paused. Then slapped him again. Eyes bled from pepper spray. Thin lines of blood seeped between the lids no breath from his teeth. Ira unzipped his fly fellow won on the Amigo. He pried open his dead mouth knelt over his face and pushed his cock between his bloody lips fucked his dead face became colder top of the inside of his mouth ridged against the soft edges of his bell-end. Ira fucked his face as Lulu fingered herself against the wall, hands inside her knickers. Ira's cock grated into the Bolivian corpse's throat cock out and wanked into his mouth and up his nostrils into the coagulating blood around his eyes. Amigo live tequila bar that's tequila. Let's get a cab back to the ship climbed over the barbed wire fence in the middle of the freeway on the other side of the dock. We could have fucking died. The cabbie wouldn't take us back to the berth. Kill three hookers in the Village and they're calling it a fucking serial killing. That made me laugh, I can fucking tell you. Old gambler stooped over his Amigo ticket shambled on the worn tile floor waitress lowered oiled asshole onto the head of Ira's cock thicker than a tube of Pringles. She eased her rectum over the bell wooden bench underneath the Amigo man hat tutted. She worked her ass back and forward over the tip of his cock he grabbed two handfuls of buttock and pulled her back and forwards she pushed four fingers into her cunt screamed. Petrol fire burned up the garage wall. Ira shat in a bag pissed in his own face cock erect balls of shit in a Sainsbury's carrier bag own face drank his own cloudy piss petrol laced flames over the side of the garage shat in a carrier bag no idea what to do with this now. Crouched in the backroom, Ira stretched Lulu's lace knickers over the head of his erection and rubbed the fabric's ridges over the edge of the head of his cock clasping the rough fabric as tight as possible over the most sensitive regions spunked lumps and pubes against the stained underwear put them into the laundry basket sat in the bath wanking two fingers up his ass took a balloon pump covered the tip perfumed soap cock sore and blotchy from lubricated masturbation. He pushed it into his ass water pumped pulled his legs up and farted it out in a thick jet flecks of pale yellow shit three times till the water ran clear. Please fuck my ass you're so tight the lubricant's doing fuck all have you ever done this before? Fingers blurred over the deg windows. Don't lie to me: have you ever done this before?

Spongy fingers coffee bonjour. We're aiming for the three fifty-eight. No hyphen dark skin cropped black hair climbed over Gérardmer towards his friends, a bright smile splitting his brown face walking stick randonnée. Swiss distorted radio Lulu sifted through systems cloud-saving. She inserted her fingertips into the window skin stripped from the bone ignited petrol crawled up the garage wall. I'm unable to suck my own cock. I've fucked everything in this house, every toilet roll, every gap between every cushion. She pulled her lips apart I don't have a condom I don't care. Ira entered from behind. She breathed heavily her lips cushioned against the pillow and the orange housing estate lighting crowed in through blue velvet curtains her asshole puckered above the top of his cock slick movement you can come inside me he pulled out and shot onto her asshole then, with great care, slotted himself into her rectum she opened her mouth against the pillow's white. He filled her ass her eyebrows knotted red damp hair piled around her cheek he came again withdrew subsided she twisted round and licked the liquids from the base of his cock, the froth of semen and spit and anal combination. Why couldn't you just wait? Screw me, she said, rubbing her clit lying on her back in the long grass on the edge of the estate streetlights thin rain fell on her freckled face. Screw me. I love the word screw. He came inside her almost immediately. Are you even on the pill? She pulled her knickers up and skipped away into the dark, pushing him back into the field's mud the back of the pub packed down behind the hedges and the main road beyond freed his cock slapped it against the top of her clit then devoured it he didn't last more than five seconds black stockings you can stick your finger up my bum, Ira. I want you to. You don't have to ask. He licked where she told him to lick and came on his face tears on the pillow. She told me she's pregnant. It isn't mine. Of course it isn't fucking yours, you cunt. Everyone knows, Ira. Everyone knows. The grey man hovered outside the room three in the morning. Are you alright? Such a baby. She visited the house and Ira hid in the loft, eating egg sandwiches and refusing to speak: such a baby. Years later he saw her driving a Metro somewhere or other, dismayed at the sight of him back in Wales. Ira the Great. Such a baby.

Entwine blue car middle of the night on the street outside her parents' house rubbed his prick through damp jeans begged to fuck 'A' levels. Of course I care I'm not the first. She drooped cream over her tits thumped up and down on his dick in the dripping tent sweat poured from her hairline down her blackhead nose and carnivore teeth worked the cream into her areolae while she violently fucked his cock sucked up his come presented her ass to him in a Hungarian tower block. I knew you'd ask. The end of the line. The sun shredded the ancient woods so far out of the city they begin to fear for their safety.

The big three, and that's too rare. Avoid the biscuits. Your teeth will fall out. Green elephant slept on a cold Roman floor shouted about cigarettes slapped the dog pasta. Basta. Platinum dye arms folded across wobbling chest, the sun long gone curly-haired hippy half-in and half-out of the tent, face crusted with sand and vomit up onto the orange mountain, green and red trucks weaving patterns against the druid stones. Destroyers ground against the invasion fleet. Are you still fucking doolaley? Let's just leave it. He cried when we went to visit him decks and powder. Wake up. No windows there apart from the glass kind can't sell the car. If he sells the car he'll have nothing left. I was looking for the bigger hit there's a library a bigger hit and it didn't fucking happen. Loon swivelled in the black leather chair retreated smile. Fuck you. Loon's third cigarette of the day. It's in the genes. Ten-packs of Marlboro combed the mouse-brown pubes of her tidy fanny on the morning of her father's funeral. Ira never returned.

Although they'd have preferred not to, the locals avoided Wrexham centre's more expensive shops. One end of the town gave over to penny arcades on a high street full of dirty jeans bent trainers three for a pound. Bimmo ploughed his Escort through Safeways' window he isn't even trying to fucking nick anything. Who's selling trips? Little Buddha. That's how he tests the whiz, innit. Just a dab. Difficult to believe he's inside in some ways, but that's it. Cat piss speed Euston Watford express. What say you, Ira? What say you, the come-down king? Adventures in tablet the clicking friendly killer out onto the Brixton street at four in the afternoon may as well have the last one. I'm peaking. I don't know what the fuck's going on. You never know what the fuck's going on, Ira. This is my holiday. The old mother hacking Birmingham hospital. Always late.

Lulu introduced Ira to her friends. They shared a house in South London fell apart trashed the black BMW in front of a speed camera came round for dinner he used to be in quite a successful band. I have to stop drinking lager with Tom. She used to be such a good friend. Lulu's face creased and the tears carved ridges in her powdered cheeks fucked to the Rocky theme. They heard it walking down the road. The heath on Hallowe'en drew the circle in the living room. Asked them in. Drank the glass of red wine in one gulp. The Leyton air static under the high ceilings traffic rolled tower block jumper over the way. Hit squad in the park. Tripped him over a football factoring bust his fucking arm red army. You've had it fucking good. You'll get your money photos of her cartwheeling across the sand, her shaved, naked genitals open in exaltation to the frigid beach. Row upon row of flowering deg. I seriously don't want to be here. Fancies himself as a drug dealer, innit. Put her in hospital lucky to survive. Warehouse nauseous

I'm going to dance deg everywhere kilos of it you look dodgy as fuck. Ira opened the bag of sticky buds, beautiful crystal on the flowers red beetles make the joints taste better, you deg? Fooking keck et, Bimmo. He keeps a gun under his pillow so would fucking I if I lived in the Park, isn't it. Eased in for five.

Carl quelled the competition with mean eyes and a roving cock. Ira never paid him back. The landlord wrote to Ira's mother demanding he be reimbursed for the rent he left without paying and quit out on the hotel in Paddington. The sniper told him it didn't matter.

Nothing ever mattered.

Chrome head sparked with starlight across the red pixies guard doors slammed shut hermetically sealed. Air free from eddies. Fourteen bodybuilders with nightsticks stripped and waiters held the doors their jockstraps deposited on silver trays. They beat Ira to the ground as he tried to escape. The Spoonfaces and the Cats hammered to be admitted held in the vacuum. The waiters didn't flinch. Ira's face exploded black batons smashed his root canals and eyes. Lulu sat cross-legged to one side sipped coffee cupped her chin in a palm. Blood squirted from his ears convulsed on the carpet spat teeth eventually his asshole wouldn't close. Lulu paid the bill bodybuilders fucked and killed each other by choking night sticks. Lulu unlocked Spoonfaces floated in the Cats remained outside as the bodybuilders evaporated into blue mist.

Ira lay dead on the carpet, worms of bloody semen crawling from his rectum down over his bare buttocks. Careful not to smear her booted foot, Lulu rolled his body over the Spoonfaces fixed in space. Ira's face flopped smashed the front of his skull flat crushed his eyes burst and leaking nose cartilage poked through ripped skin. You make me so angry. Go away. I don't want you.

You're so unapproachable. I'm doing fucking admin, trying to get on with my life. Earn money. Independent. Lulu chewed her nails over Ira as blood oozed from his wounds. The Cats made a terrible racket with their crying the Spoonfaces poofed into green smoke and burned through a window barely large enough to admit a dragonfly. Escape became impossible. Ira and Lulu raced through the smoking basement hands in desperate links. Don't look through the windows. Cadarves screamed into their ears dragged Ira through the flames neck stuck in the window Scottish bull licked his asshole. I know you're a fucking artist. Fuck off post to feed optional waited for the green tick Lulu blew oxygen into Ira's dead lungs blood and spit smeared across her cheeks tears blinded her ball-bearing eyes. Loon touched her on the shoulder. She turned and hugged him. I'm going to see if I can pay over the phone. Why don't you just go to the bank?

A vista of white and gold gravestones. Lulu and Loon searched the names holes in the wall Cadarves earpieces but too late for Ira. He didn't see that coming, being dead and all daunting. What are you doing for your seventieth? Lulu flicked the roach onto the churned earth war graves tumbled through the mosquito afternoon. Lulu exhaled columns of deg smoke into the sunlight. Why do you have to get so fucking angry? Cadarves picked at his boot and coloured the florist blue stroked the hills. Loon here he is. That's all fine. So you drive to the ferry. I see. Lulu connected the network installed security took his leave and booked a one-way trip to the star bridges. Loon didn't complain. You should call my father. I'm afraid he refuses to pay and this is all a little embarrassing. You're not wrong, he said.

We drove back but no stops presented themselves, and Ira admitted he'd reached the end of that particular road. He lorded over the opposite edge of Trafalgar Square shut the American right up. I'm less than pleased with his performance. The highest license is only achievable through wall-bouncing. Meat. He came down from the Midlands regularly meat twenty double vodkas your mates were spiking you. You didn't ring on the fucking doorbell, did you? You fucking tool. My baby's asleep up there. It's a draw. Iron gloves spread noses across brain-damaged faces. I know you're a fucking artist. I know what I'm doing I'm just too embarrassed to admit it. If you've got a great body just feels a little tight around here, she said, gesturing towards her vagina. You need to get down to a size ten if you want to wear the decent suits, you know.

I know, she said.

Wind pumpkin the smell of fires and rotting oak leaves a bell that never rings anymore been in use since the Middle Ages. Call the police: hooligans in the graveyard. Whooping cough on the streets of Camden twenty quid a pipe. You can't even clean knee socks preened in the pub mirror juddered full of arcing electricity against transparent skin. Ear and nose and lip piercings ghostly faces and bare legs brimming with blue fire twitched down the street selling shit weed to tourists. Deg in flames. Bright green poured over the white lines electro-twitchers filled the markets and the World's End spilled out into the tube buying bottles of vodka to fill the platforms, vomit spraying the stairs streams of blue lasers connecting the knee socks down under London high. Touch your hair in the mirror. Take a look in the fucking glass. Deg panes maintained form for milliseconds on kerbs. We'll be back soon. Loon and Ira programmed the fire-women from Earl's Court's command centre. Flat face screens cracked their brains leaked on the shit-strewn flags of West Cromwell Road.

I can't maintain the porn streams, said Loon crushed handkerchief dabbed his forehead as he reached for the plug.

Cadarves snickered and vanished through the blue door into the white stairwell void cream stars flattened out into the London night. Waves of explosions barred the exits. Drink your beer and shut up. Rioters smashed car windows as cops snarled beneath armour burned Robin Reliants back from Goodge Street threw bricks through McDonald's window the deg tube tide diminished under a typhoon of pepper spray and armoured vehicles. Maybe next time, boys? Anarchy has failed, spat the racist. Working class movement I don't agree with you there. You knew about this. Read between the lines. Paris shoed back on the Tuileries Garden CRS removed deg heads to cells for final processing. Cash registers rang feebly but with increasing passion as the deg tubes collapsed down the Seine to Notre Dame. Ira and Lulu beer cocktail nearly snapped his dick drunk back in the train carriage resto. Do you have a cigar for me? The waiter slapped him across the face too full to drink more.

Last few euros slapped nightstick onto palm just half-baked idealism student logic incapable of making anything stick. First we'll take out the trains and then fucking what? Minimum trouble for the maximum amount of people. You aren't big enough to be able to look after yourself. Blood traced over the top of Ira's eyebrow and down onto his lip. His wrists felt as though they approached snapping handcuffed to the metal chair. No light droids circled assembled in infrared occasionally probed his ears and eyes transmitted thought eradication processes dragged him face-down across cobbles reached inside to remove his spleen. Lulu fled to Brazil with Jimmy the Weasel, joined Loon on the other side let me tell you a story. I fought in Bosnia over the favela toothless man one leg begged for bread. I fought in Bosnia, he said, and we raped a woman. She'd just given birth, so her cunt was slack. One of my sergeants tightened her up real quick by slicing the infant to pieces in front of her. We all took turns. We killed her after we'd finished. It didn't seem right to let her live.

When I first started out I was angry, but I'm not angry anymore. Loon refused to make eye contact. There's no place for you in this organisation, he said, looking down at his fingers clacking over the keyboard implants connection cloud window this is the new age. Why use deg to achieve flat screens? First draft deg arcs archaic, and I haven't seen Cadarves for years. He's probably dead. He pushed out from Brazil into Peru. You know how it is.

Pearly teeth you can put them back on. Belgrade tower blocks buggered him in front of his friends. They bent him over a bench and forced his friends to watch cried for their mothers they never did that again. Blue hands amber skin sucked the deg out of the ice bong, the tourists packing around the window five euro if you want to watch. Doughnutting in the Outback we'll fucking kill you. Take a crowbar and push you into the sand and cave your skull into your fucking neck. No one will find you out here, boy. Ira believed them.

Earth reddened places will become uninhabitable sustained wet bulb above 35°C lethal hyperthermia. My father taught me how to use a gun throw a spear deg collapsed the Turbo Town plantation tattered nothing left to grow. This is how you load a magazine. This is how you arm it. This is how you point it. This is how you pull the trigger. This is how you kill.

We want Lunar Jim boots disturbed the moon's surface launch detected. NASA upped its fourth manned transport in as many months. Central global regions full carbon dispersal. Russian drones recycled CO2 lack of funding. Human female liquid metal suit screen moulded over her face embraced young child as Earth filled white horizon. Cellular structures fusion plant drank recycled urine strip lights in the rear corridor for the deg Russian drones US effort more than a billion floating face down in the acid sea, the fires in London and Paris wisps of smoke into the subways. Ira choked to death. Mercury suit feedback to support drones capable of withstanding Pluto conditions. Gravity drove outer asteroid plastic mining we'll fucking kill you. That can never be a real fish wild Alaskan salmon really is superior. Do you want some butter with that? Some cream cheese? You got up earlier than me experienced the same levels of addiction low-lying countries heat stress 2100 increase limits were a fucking fairytale. We didn't need to burn anything. Money did it decades before.

Lulu stretched a platinum leg out over the waterfall, electric blue etching its surface violet reflecting from the lagoon. Ira hovered out over a chasm full of pink spray searched down for the four-by-four burned at the bottom of the cliff razors slashed green dogs in the pit below resurrected by blue fire. He converted to green through deg filters reputation back against the wall. What are you going to do, man? Pushed for the sixty wet bulb time for planting.

Spade hit the red pipes clay mud traps waterproof trousers purple forested hills flicked emerald lighting on the planets sector past the star bridges. Spoonfaces and Cats holidayed on the gas moons. Ira dug dog fertilizer into satellite mud. Gas suckers built windmills in the methane hurricanes, fire disasters dropping twelve megatons backside the ultra-flames. A roar up the genus nothing through you to the stars buried in your eyes, my love. Ira's face expanded upwards and downwards. His arms shrank up into his body as bitter roots wound down into white dust through his toes, roots reaching out from his shiny concave face now you are the Spoonfaces launched their ether vessels down from chooner moon and Ira beamed out Cat noise from the propane wells. Lulu sprouted fur ears grew up as Ira aimed the signal through her sinuses out to the potato fields on the upside quango, beef in the chicken mouse. The Spoonfaces drifted down through diamond semen. The Cats accelerated fusion bolts multiplied twenty-eight thousand light removed half the planet with a sullen gesture. Ira and Lulu accepted their place with the Spoonfaces and entered singularity. The star bridges winked out, relegated to the past.

Sores of pink and green organic brick reappeared after splitting the methane carrots took out many of the Cats in the great bridge disaster. Cat disaster. Ira and Lulu hugged all the way back to Earth. Loon, however, tapped his stained fingers on the café table. What time do you call this? We're quite busy. Blue balls on the carbonised mudflats won't work, you know. Lock it up drop it in the sea encase it in lead receipt for the German hotel turned his leg inside out. Lulu delved into the mines. Strasbourg cathedral you make a good couscous. If two people can't see eye-to-eye, why inflict the nightmare on their children? Why stay with one person for the rest of your life? Better for everyone Tunisia at school but I stopped.

They speak French all over North Africa. We can watch Tunisian TV in Cairo. I can't leave the house at the moment. It isn't safe. Deg tubes corkscrewed and collapsed anemone. Ira cleared Turbo Town's streets with loops of glass coiled around his head situation and memory tidal his hair constantly returning to the same sentences no escape. He tore at the tubes. Globules of glitter glue sprayed from his head green and ruby gems smashed the Turbo windows showered tourists open mouths filled with wallpaper paste internal hungry mouths sucked it up this can't. Ira tottered and crumpled next to the carousel. Call les gendarmes. Schoolgirl bus stabbing admitted land of hope hated Britain. He hated Britain. As pointless as loving it. The Tunisian lit a cigarette and waved to Ira from his bike as he dodged red ice.

TEN ———

An awkward splinter from a picnic bench overlooked black Cat nettled horny goats blocked the path dust nowhere to park. Be gentle with the Cat, remember mewed next to the colouring block while the boys argued over felt-tips and sharpeners. I'm going to get it black hats and jodhpurs, young dusty women running across the farmyard bonjour. The Cat settled opened silver window white sunlight ruffled through its fur and it squinted at Ira, batting its ears at the children's chatter. Mother and daughter scowled down from the carpark, stick thin and hard, both dressed in black. Pink legs ça va, Florence, Lucky Strike chessboard mare up by blue-top under the water tower coloured a baby red with a blue bottle. The Cat, older than Ira first thought, hunched over the valley as an anorak mother drew champagne from a plastic bag and her ponytailed girl grabbed for sandwiches. Motes branches tail twitched nettles sang in the October breeze gardens still full of vegetables. Elle est malade. White Cat cows wine pop and an old man tongued an electronic cigarette. The boy gaped on. He threw all his pens to the floor joyeux anniversaire. Two teenage girls red hair grey torn t-shirts black jodhpurs kissed in the stable doorway, long black hair purple vest stick thin teased a goat by holding its horns making it butt her in the thighs all laughed filthy boots Paisley socks pulled over trouser bottoms. Lulu and Ira. I don't think the two of us should come here together anymore. Horses Channel waves necks kicked up dust. Distant ache of jet planes golden sun diffuse.

Flat shoes instructor whipped over sand. Proud slim dark girl gripped the reins in the stable, dust infusing the air like sugar in tea. Milky forest. The teacher urged Ira's daughter to trot, but she refused. Just a little hole where her friend used to be. A wheelbarrow full of shit three wasps. Dark-haired son sat at a picnic table sketched in his cahier. The twins set up in their riding helmets the boss, a little stricter than the other lady, but the daughter refused to accelerate. She enjoyed swimming, but part of her didn't want to make the effort with sport. I don't believe that, said Ira. White donkey scratched behind the ears tan goat chewed over his beard lay on the cracked mud. Two of the older girls tended to a fine duff mare black pink pig swept up the edges of the farmyard flicked human eyes. La nature est fragile stable sign batted away wasps empty sty. The black pig made itself immovable. Ira noted its tusks look at them there. Look at them sat down stayed there. He's a machine. Don't pull out the middle of the plant. We've had some complaints about the cauliflowers being bruised. Hacked the heads from the fields with curved blades felt hats protected them from bare sun. I don't like queuing for anything. London was a bit of a shock, I can tell you. We rested under a banyan eating bread and cheese salad sandwiches arcing water inked the sky bluer. There's a Scandinavian only flew in a week ago his arm couldn't survive a single session. Sydney burned flames seared crowd faced melting the children raised their hands and tittered.

ELEVEN ———

Cold out the back of the school. Frames for climbing boards for walking. Over the field, toothy against an inverted sunset, the Le Lonzac cemetery little ballerinas pretended to be birds in bay windows. Mirrored glass Ira against the low grey wall electrician's son opposite afro chatted about Disneyland c'est pas cher staying for four days, he said, although Ira, as ever, had difficulty understanding. Glass copper patina glazed the graves. Three fifty for a Perrier. Do you know of anywhere to rent in the village? Sit, monsieur, sit at the bar would you like to join us a coffee, please shoulder length black hair lost weight looks great, said Lulu, and she took the time to talk to Ira when he dropped her daughter off from the dance class. He asked in improving French whether or not she'll see her father at the weekend or during the holidays and the two girls blathered in the back about horses and how difficult maternelle to primaire to collège to lycée. Toy horses. They giggled behind the driver minus-six ice-crusted sun struggled above the white pines turned this way and that but never had he seen such woods. Trees in every direction forever, no marker or term of distinction like swimming in the deep sea out to a platform off the Greek coast, wherever it was, a pontoon for diving in the Adriatic on the west side the ferry over from Brindisi well-made from barrels and rope. They took it in turns to swim underneath wearing their only mask, Ira and Jacob, muscular near black with tan sea water shone on their tight skin like jewels. Ira held onto the barrels swam face down and below him the platform's tether descended into the water beyond sight bent by the current. Rays of sunlight rose back up from a central unseen point somewhere at the bottom of the sea. Water darker further down and no features no specks just an endless milled blue of atoms and light unseen monsters in the deep. Ira's heart swelled blue at the sight of it and he was unable to stay under the water for too long. Jacob's cock flopped between his legs stretched out on the platform's bleached surface, tight foreskin pinching the bell trim pubes. Only the grey deep in the trees no end to the trunks and no sign of the steel clouds beyond. Blue patches overhead cold bit down pinching the extremities of his hands and ears. No compass or phone, only a locking combat knife clasped onto the top of his frayed jeans pocket. He flicked it open no way of contacting Lulu clean as linen paling to darkness miles from the gîte. His car lost to the green next to the wood mountain split boots crunched the beginnings of ice. Moss sucked at his feet laughed wanted to eat him down into the thick sheets of broken trunks on which no one had stood for decades. If ever the deg fields that never were or ever would be a quad parked in the bottom of a ravine so deep Ira chattered to himself and sized-up trees and hollows if his irresponsibility forced to sleep in the woods for the night, to use the knots he learned on YouTube and his laces to string a bivvy. He circled the bike searched the trees grasped the knife in his right palm scanned the trunks for the owner. Footsteps broke for cover hid twenty feet back dead still bulky hunter in camouflage wore a webbing facemask a crossbow black quiver bounced from his thigh. He paused by the bike and squinted over the top of the language more guttural than he would have liked. The parlance of the normal person is unlike anything you learn in a classroom. My sister is twenty-eight years old call her mobile and say bonjour maybe speak a few words to her in English. She likes England a lot. She goes there on holiday a lot. You have a permit not yet monsieur it's hard three years for a carte vitale started the engine kicked up leaf mulch as he skidded away. Ira jerked himself behind the bush immaculate suit red pocket handkerchief limped with a stick sirop à l'eau followed the quad trails then veered back up the cliff over the valley summit hit another path moon sang overhead. The temperature cratered. He sought a place to warm no chance of making a fire here and nothing to light it with. Take your coat off lay it on the ground Gresford phone number sprinkled a thick layer of dry leaves over the lining then put it back on lie on the ground roll up in as many leaves as you can a good way of trapping heat set of muddy headlights pricked the track hick pick-up and they stopped next to him in a growl in brakes. He concealed the knife behind his back.

Je peux vous aider?

Je suis perdu.

Evidement, monsieur.

Je cherche ma voiture.

They scowled at him from behind the blotched windscreen, eyes whiter than eggs skin black as sheep next to the cabbage patch last sprouts of the year thick with frost shone in the darkness. He told them he parked his car next to the wood mountain but wasn't able to make them understand asked directions back to Treignac vouz arrivez but it isn't possible, they said.

Ira climbed into the back of truck. Initially they kept the door closed but he rubbed his crotch and they flicked the lock. Weevil beards and waxy ears, frayed caps dull in the deep dusk. Ruts bounced back from headlights mud track four-by-four Border Collie black white howled at the men as they passed through the gate into the lightless farm. Crescent empty black severed an outhouse door. Full moon dribbled down from the onyx winter night stars pigs and goats snuffled awake in their sties. The horses snorted clouds of steam from stable doors carriage flat tyre in the blank face of the Corrèzian farmhouse sparked granite minusten. Ira bought bread in the boulangerie the old timers drooped eyes nodded to each other. Ça commence. Sheets of ice crystals staccato on the webbed windows snapped bare bulb on the inside. Ira went to make some coffee without being asked.

Filthy jeans and a buttonless suit jacket clung to Pierre, the older of the two French farmers. He rubbed the neck of his stinking purple t-shirt. The other, Matthieu, shuffled his belly and wore oily overalls all messy from fixing a cam on the big green tractor earlier in the day. They both said they wanted coffee and Ira put it on then leant up against the kitchen surface his cock escaping the top of his jeans throbbed painful balls swollen and purple. Pierre and Matthieu shifted in silence under the hissing bulb not a stroke of wind outside in the deep freeze. Ira unzipped his trousers a few centimetres black eyes and the two Frenchmen began to undress. Ira took his cock out the zip of his jeans abrasive against the shaft's shaved base. Fat Matthieu out of his overalls in a white t-shirt splattered with sweat and a pair of blue underpants. He creaked to his knees curly hair ten-day stubble furry gut dropped from the bottom of his t-shirt down onto his thighs ran his white tongue around the head of Ira's cock, all round the purple rim. He tickled his balls with his grimy hands. Ira grabbed his greasy ringlets and pushed himself past rotten teeth. He clamped his lips onto the shaft and coated the bell in brown tobacco saliva. Pierre loaded a pump-action shotgun while Ira fucked Matthieu's mouth. Pierre took a green plastic cartridge and the shotgun rattled on the pine kitchen table. He pushed the shell into Matthieu's ass failed to insert into his rectum held it up to the light spat on it great gob smeared it over the plastic casing with calloused fingers bent down again and successfully fitted. Matthieu groaned began to chew Ira's cock bit it hard Ira grabbed his hair again forced his length into Matthieu's throat and refused to let him breath. Matthieu blew snot through his crusty nose. Pierre removed the cartridge covered in grommets of hairy shit. He loaded it into the shotgun. Ira released his hair Matthieu spluttered back vomited with a smile Ira stepped over to the table bent over so his cock down to his knees hung over the edge towards the floor. He stretched his arms forward and grabbed the other side. Matthieu rose from the floor muddy thin long cock dripping with smegma the yellow crust cracked the surface underneath a blood-streaked liquid coated the inside of his foreskin smeared it over his fingers sniffed and used it to lubricate Ira's asshole. Pierre pushed a beetroot into Ira's ass relaxed. Pierre eased the root fully into his asshole, dragged himself round the other side of the table. Matthieu spanked Ira's ass with the end of his stinking cock. Pierre retrieved the shotgun and used the butt to crush Ira's fingers against the table planks bucked. Ira screamed. Matthieu grabbed the protruding beetroot big as a tennis ball yanked it rectum prolapsed. Pierre punched Ira's broken fingers. Ira's ass hung out over the back of his thigh Mathieu played with it with his fat dirty hands grabbed a handful and pulled down tore it away in a shower of blood and shit pulled again tore it from his body. Ira's legs uncontrolled spasm. Pierre hooted and danced in circles at the far end of the table, slapping the end of his cock with his encrusted fingers singing songs about the moon and the bears and the wolves and the bison. Ira white area ascension. Pierre grabbed a bread knife. Matthieu hammered fencing staples through Ira's hands to the table steel blood flowed over the rust red tiles small and large intestines poked through the Matthieu hefted down on his anus ripping a large hole the rest of his guts start to poke through bread knife carved away his buttocks. Ira pleaded to the Spoonfaces no answer sliced through the fat and muscle of the larger part of his ass shrivelling cock. Matthieu sucked Ira's balls into his mouth slick with blood and shit and bit through the tissue took his time ground the tubes and skin between his teeth crunched on the testicles. Ira buzzed high frequency skin shone green. Pierre fired shots into the kitchen ceiling ejecting the shells pushing them into Ira's mouth eyes full of tears saw nothing unable to make sounds other than abattoir grunting. Matthieu chewed through Ira's scrotum cut off his cock with the bread knife. Pierre shot Ira in the leg it near enough fell off point-blank range with a twelve-bore slug. They found this extremely funny. Ira smiled and offered up his thanks then clutched his black coat around his chest and rested his pint of lager on the varnished shelf. Approached two skinheads hidden faces we're from Newcastle fifteenth pint how about I pick you up and throw you off the fucking balcony there? Come on, mate. Why don't you fuck off? You fuck her in the ass payment up front. You sit there. Have you paid already? Don't touch the condom, she yelled Eastern Europe unable to maintain anything but a sausage-soft erection. She pulled the thick rubber down over his dick which sucked up some more blood pubes stank don't touch the condom windows twitched in the corner he's really pissed have you paid yet oh baby oh oh oh baby she bounced ineffectually on the head of his dwindling cock. Ira covered his face with yellow hands. Oh baby. Was that good for you?

Ira found his jeans wet with rancid sweat out into the sitting area. Loon flinched on a threadbare couch under a middle-eastern gentleman white shirt hairless pushed to feed have you paid yet? How was it? Loon Aryan white emerged five minutes later fag packets on the carpet need something else? We just need somewhere to drink. I know a place you can drink till the sun comes up let's go. Piss-rank alleys this way you can drink forever. Come this way with me I think we should just keep going got any back-up? Yeah, a bit hey where the fuck are you going? Hey, come back. Hey, you ever come down here again I'll kick your fucking ass. Never come back here. Never come back go back send them back. Theresa May go home secretary Topfluffer non-existent benefit tourism sarahditum the more Labour has apologised for its record on immigration, the more the myth has taken hold that we promoted uncontrolled immigration HackneyAbbott Theresa May: I don't think illegal immigrants should be able to open bank accounts. I don't think you can think thejimsmith. Are you white, Stefan? Are you white? There are no black faces on the FN website, are there? Are you white? Marine Le Pen: Il y a incontestablement une poussée assez spectaculaire du FN qui est enregistrée élection après élection. Rolls of flame licked at the green avenues of Paris and London.

The window flexed and shattered.

Ira pulled his hands away from his eyes to find them dripping with blue blood she shouldn't really put that on there, should she? Lulu chewed a piece of green cheese locked up the window with fuzzy matches. The rue dissolved whipped apart through the perennial incapacity vortex a field of seagulls munched up the stalks corn sprayed out triple light speed event horizon splintered on the Exxon Valdez whales don't need serving breakfast. I'm pretty sure they've finished now. Ira tried to remove the American woman's plate bought him a keyring. They held hands pranced down the yellow tunnel to the dining room. It'd be good if you could sit us with some nice Jewish people tonight. Ira laughed but the bejewelled diners didn't. Next time you come down here maybe you bring a little something. It helps. Ira opened his palm to reveal a Swiss Army knife he brought with him through Montreal and the Asians laughed, slapped him on the back shook their heads you ever try it with a guy? Hair extensions pumped arms loaded cargo for the ship's freezers. If you're late for service you get sent to the hold for lifting. New York showed his bruised arms to the maître d' the rest laughed nice haircut. You have a little colour in your cheeks you did a great job with that. Fuck, man, he's a fucking faggot. The Dutchman ketchup hotdog sure we're going to do some coke, Bean. Sure we're going to do some coke.

Will you call my sister? She really wants to speak some English. I'll never forgive that fucking Dutch cunt get off the ship let's see if we can get you something nice to do in Montreal. No, said Ira. I'm going to tough it out.

Fortune eased down onto his erection belly button piercing banging against the top of her pubis brown asshole opening and contracting in front of the mirror. Lulu up against the mattress in an alley near Highbury tube drunk groans black night man loitered. Ira fucked her against the vertical cloth cut off the deg loop reattached to alter circumstance files through the outzone.

Nera and Javi slid to a halt at the end of the piste. The little girl refused to trot. She wouldn't learn to ski jump. Ira regularly forgot to articulate his pride at her French and English, of her swimming badminton horse riding stared at the bedroom ceiling rehearsed lines he'd never say. We both love you. He closed the door on the elephant. We're both so proud of you. I'll just put that out there. Ira said nothing in response.

The little boys beamed gut-wrenching thrill as the horses moped past one waved the other grabbed Ira's finger. I'm running out of fuel. Down to Mexico. She lives in Nuremburg. She's married to a German. I am a king of the road. Leaves fell breathing with difficulty. Lulu firmed as the frequency of her swimming increased joined the society ran on the Parcour de Santé back in the woods managed thirty minutes fitter than she thought, her arms pumping against the slate pines. She made Ira run the entire way back with a cèpe. I didn't want to give it to anyone else. They embraced and she ensured he sat on a towel for the drive home.

Now hear this. I got a brand new car. I drove into the middle of town, down into Colmar, and went prepared on this occasion armed with several windows and a sledgehammer. I tied him to the bed in a bedsit I rented using a false passport three months beforehand. Cadarves helped with that. I tied him to the bed he let me because he thought he was about to get his cock sucked. Cock wet called an escort Adam slumped on the other side of the table six pints of Stella to the bad. He looked sheepish, but didn't refuse. Steve made a show of getting ready to call a hooker but that was Steve: total load of shit.

I stripped him off and strapped him down. Up bounced the thickest cock I'd ever seen. Straight up, the guy was a fucking monster. Must have been ten inches long and wider than a TV remote quite difficult to get even the end of it into my mouth. Ouvrez votre bouche serrez les dents. Gym sweat stench rose from his ass. Ira pushed his mouth over the head bare bulb moths flitted around cheap wallpaper green stained with damp patches managed to get his teeth over the lip of the bell and nibbled the Arab crooned. Naam, he repeated. Ira removed his mouth left a string of green spit. Arab strained against the restraints eyes widened as Ira strolled into the one-flush bathroom and returned with the sledgehammer. He dangled it over his head. The Arab scrunched up his eyes and turned his face to the side. Ira dropped it onto the side of his head he barked in Arabic. Ira dropped it onto his face repeatedly until his cheekbone broke. His eyes swivelled in his dark face alternating white black wrists tugged at the blue cords plastic got them from a garden centre the previous week skinning knife and sliced off one of his nipples pissed on the wound crouched over his face and shat on him left for the evening and shut the door locked it. The new car purred back up to Gérardmer took dinner with Lulu. A nice lamb rack. Mint jelly.

She returned with him to Colmar the following day. Burning him isn't an option you're getting ahead of yourself. Let's go shopping and wait till he calms down. The Christmas market Glühwein in the snow arm-in-arm stalls sold dried meats and toys for the children. Mother's coming for Christmas. She's landing at Basel. You have to be sure you don't step over onto the Swiss side. This sent her into a tizz. The stench of vomit and faeces leaked from the door as they entered the bedsit and dropped the shopping bags in the bathroom. Lulu scraped Ira's old turd from the side of the Arab's face. He mumbled and cried. She used Ira's shit to lubricate the Arab's cock which became erect not entirely sure if he can see anything the right side of his face badly discoloured and swollen from Ira's sledgehammer. Good meeting with Iraqi Speaker @Osama_Alnujaifi on importance of 2014 elections and political progress to address instability @WilliamJHague fat cock thick with shit Lulu managed to take the entire thing into her ass a ring of shit collected around her asshole as she slid down the length. Ira slapped her clit as she fucked the Arab came in her rectum. She raised herself off and her ass didn't close. The Arab's spunk dripped down her inner thigh mixed with shit. Let's just leave him here, she said, kissing his swollen forehead. I doubt it'll take long.

Ira's tombstone creaked in the wind. Beech leaves floated down behind cover the turned earth deer jerked this way and that along the caravan, a bus full of deg smokers and stashes of tiles. The Vézère rushed further along the track. Beech and oak stood together the winter colourless, dank. Ira slowed his sessions dressed like a dandy for the lake runs, dropped from four to three and bought himself a neat pair of swimming trunks. He got himself some new tattoos in Strasbourg. Cheese sandwich shop in Colmar little boys ice skated learned to bend down move forward one of them cried his face scrunched up too tired. Enough for today. The little blonde girl bounced from the library room, all teeth and eyes, waving a piece of stiff paper onto which she'd smeared oil crayons and glue. She hugged her daddy, who praised her and kissed the top of her head. Fifty centimes from the tooth fairy. It's a mouse in France Grandma's coming for Christmas. I very well may not be here before too long, Ira, she said on the drive back to the airport. We're still waiting for the snow learn to ski. I had a wonderful time. So did we, said Ira.

Ira and Lulu sang Cat on the windowsill snow toffee swung into the café and took a table, slipped their coats off and relaxed onto the hard wooden benches. Une petite crème et un café, said the waiter bald podgy man about forty-five smiled and said salut. I like it in here, said Lulu. It's my favourite coffee and biscuits packs of sugar they never used faced each other swiped their windows getting bigger omg haha ashamed by the typo Facebook distraction from the subconscious hole in your pride. Lulu complained about dictionary installation database management sipped her milky coffee while Ira read an article in French about the rise of Marine and fought fascists on Twitter. Cadarves hovered near the door but Ira and Lulu ignored him as ill-conceived. He exited into the thin snow and headed up to the piste.

Deg1 nothing left but icy stalks the main crop unused in the Paris London assault shipped into Switzerland for cash money, gringo. They'll never turn you back at the border assuming you have something they can sell window will charge you five euro just to step inside the country after Schengen possible to drive to the top of Sweden without ever showing a passport. Cadarves buried the papers under Deg2. The Cats patted him on the back showed their brown teeth bloody eyes. Switzerland decriminalised deg and Cadarves shrugged his shoulders, trudged down through the snow and back to the café. Lulu and Ira had already left.

It's going to be tight, you know, said Ira showing Lulu the map. Hotel de la Paix no need to go that way I only have half an hour got to get the boys ready after their swimming creative class. Ira sat at the window Reddit Facebook Twitter traffic sales email digital loop circles out on the stars crammed with cocksuckers licked the frizzy pussy. The windows enlarged. Infographic of rock concerts from the sixties to present day eventually showed photos Reddit Facebook Twitter ten-inch iPads circles groaned under data weight. Frizzy hair moulded the corner of her lipstick and turned her back when Ira came close. He spoke to an underling about his job and went to buy more coffee.

Cadarves didn't remove his coat until Lulu invited him to do so. Ira stood from the table and shook his hand, offering him a seat. How've you been? Lulu mixed a drink. Cadarves shrugged and skinned up from a rolling tobacco pouch yellow fingers and bristles. The snow fell with greater conviction beyond the black windows and Ira moved the wireless thermostat to the coldest section of the house to bring the temperature up pumped out warmer from the oil tank. It's fine. Don't worry about it. Lulu distributed some mulled wine and Ira stroked her thigh, watched Cadarves's eyes track his fingers. Anti-fog.

Chicken all right for you? asked Ira. Cadarves passed him the joint.

Sure, he replied, rubbing his stubble.

I cooked it earlier, said Ira. It has olives and peppers.

He's a good cook, Lulu said to Cadarves. He nodded and prepared another joint sipped his spice and crossed his wiry legs. The Christmas tree twinkled behind the candles.

Ira chewed the smoke, but he could sense the beginnings of a growth in the top of his lung borrowed time. Could be stopped if he bought himself a new pair of swimming goggles and contemplated for the first time a future without deg. Lulu pushed for it, complained about applications for a while then settled into German French English directed dissertation southern border with Italy. Why don't you move down there if you like it? No, we're fine where we are. Ira's father looked away.

I've been considering buying some blotters from Silk Road ultimate window busted for organising hit. Unable to maintain tabs on all Tor users window disappeared from the Paris failure.

Cadarves licked the paper and rolled the joint, his eyes sparkling at the MDMA rocks. It's never going to stop, you know, he said to Ira, and poured out some brandy. They wiped the chicken tomato olive juices from their plates with campagne crusts. If it isn't us collapse. Yeah, said Ira. It's all Grand Theft this and Watch Dogs that. Even the frizzer's calmed down. Cadarves lit the spliff half a bottle of brandy and they laughed the snow cast spells. Christmas lights rotated from blue to carbon hot. Clouds of green smoke hugged each other. They pushed back onto the settee and giggled into the silent flakes.

Author photo courtesy of **Laura Stevens**
http://www.laurastevens.co.uk/portraits

Patrick Garratt is a writer and journalist with a long history of covering technology and video games. His work has been published by *The Sunday Times, The Huffington Post, The Independent* and *The Face*.

He tweets @patlike.

Find more information at his website: http://patrickgarratt.com/

Urbane Publications is dedicated to developing new author voices, and publishing fiction and non-fiction that challenges, thrills and fascinates.

From page-turning novels to innovative reference books, our goal is to publish what YOU want to read.

Find out more at
urbanepublications.com